The Blue Stoop
-A New Orleans Novella-

Zack O'Neill

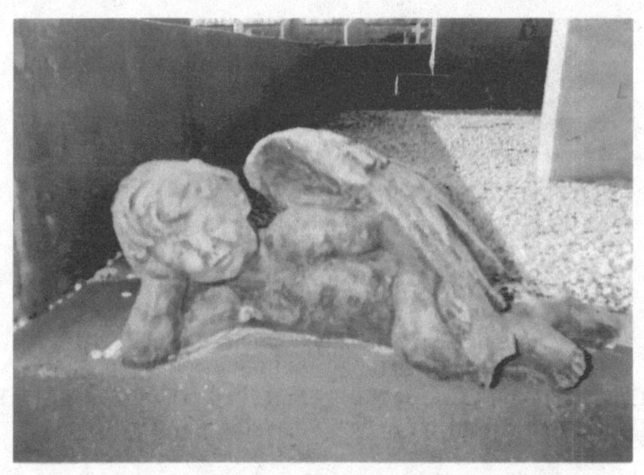

Spuyten Duyvil

New York City

© 2019 Zack O'Neill
ISBN 978-1-949966-45-9

Library of Congress Cataloging-in-Publication Data

Names: O'Neill, Zack, author.
Title: The blue stoop / Zack O'Neill.
Description: New York City : Spuyten Duyvil, [2019]
Identifiers: LCCN 2019020124 | ISBN 9781949966459
Classification: LCC PS3615.N49 B58 2019 | DDC 813/.6--dc23
LC record available at https://lccn.loc.gov/2019020124

"Like a blighted fruit tree he shook, and cast his last,
cindered apple to the soil"

ISHMAEL

1.

Looking back, I thought:

As the car pulled up headlights blinded me.

The driver's window rolled down.

"Adam?"

I nodded.

The back door opened.

Four guys I didn't know were inside. None of them Andrew.

No one spoke as we went up Dumaine, left on Rampart, across Canal, left on Poydras, right on Tchoupitoulas. On one block in the Warehouse District a bunch of kids ran around a spraying fire hydrant. Our driver, whoever he was, leaned on the horn. They were slow to move, just staring at us, curious. Some of them were naked.

-

From the get-go I was raking, and it felt good to be back behind big chip cylinders, but I felt off, self-conscious, worried about an unseen bad beat, tells, my slump. Considering the aftermath, of course, the wins were just more bad luck. I should have known: tense atmosphere, not much talk aside from Andrew's occasional joke. I should have seen how the strangers, Andrew's forced ebullience, the quietude, and the giant empty apartment with the blinds drawn gave the whole thing a stench of predetermination. Fixedness.

When Andrew busted out he flashed his toothy smile and made a self-effacing joke about his poker skills while some kid pulled the chips in. He didn't acknowledge me as he stood, took out his phone, checked it, shook some hands. Not even a glance before he turned and left.

This was the real Genesis of the story. Or the myth perversion, depending on which of the patterns you subscribed to, apple-tree, or ocean cycles.

As the game went on I sank into myself, tried to not want things so much, occupied my mind with something trivial. That's how I always calmed myself. I went to a memory of being at the western end of a highway that connects oceans. A long time ago I'd run into a kid there, someone who could play, who had endurance and knew what he was doing. Skinny kid. Hard stare, still as a statue, betokening nothing. This was at a casino out in Gardena. A long time ago.

At *that* game, as the night pushed on, the deals came out, the players came and went, the slot machines beeped and jingled and the luck moved back and forth pretty evenly between he, I, all the strays that'd come and go in the blink of an eye. In time, we became comfortable. Settled. Or at least he did.

"How long you been here?" he said to me during a hand we'd both folded out of.

"At the table?"

"No, I mean *here*," he said, gesturing vaguely at everything around us.

"Oh," I said. "Well, not too long I guess."

"Live close by?"

"No I don't. From way down the road."

He was quiet.

"How about you?" I said.

"Santa Monica."

"Really?"

"Right on the beach," he said.

"Nice. You must like these games a lot to be all the way out here."

"I have a friend in the Coast Guard," he said, shifting in his chair, "who told me how they find people who drown in the surf."

"Oh yeah?"

"See, the currents move in circular patterns."

He demonstrated with his hand.

"Out on the shelf, in the shallows," he said, "the currents catch people and carry them around in circles. To find them, the Coast Guard sets up three or four boats in the path of the circle. They go back and forth, over and over, until one of their boats crosses paths with the body."

"Is that right?"

"They use boats less now because of sonar. Of course, they still miss them sometimes. The things lose their buoyancy and sink after a few days, and sometimes they fall out of the pattern and drift to deeper waters, where the sharks are. They like to lurk in the underwater canyons, you know."

"The sharks do, you mean."

He looked confused.

"Right," he said. "The sharks."

I smiled.

Later, I imagined drifting down into an underwater canyon, with frowning sharks swimming up to me and thrusting one eye forward, others swirling all around me in the cobalt light. Looking up, I'd see the surface of the sea, a turquoise gleam getting smaller, the boats gliding back and forth, cutting the glassy surface open.

Below my feet, something dark would be coming up. Something slow. Massive. Rising to meet me.

2.

It was the bells—not the murmurs, hand claps, footsteps, techno jams, boat bleats, or even muleclops that clip-tocked over every goddamned second of my half-sleep, but the fugue of rusty rattle-clangs from the quasidiluvian cathedral that woke me. I sat up, felt air rush through my nostrils, pain in my ribcage, head, feet. Nausea. A fat old couple walked by. They looked at me like I was a leper. I leaned forward, grinned at them, and said in a child-molester voice, "You guys like to get high?" and they scurried off like roaches in sudden light.

My immediate environment was more benches, briar nettles, grass, dandelions, iron gates, drooping tree branches that dangled above the gates like fingers over piano keys.

Between the rooted populace and iron-wrought frippery, you had

fortune tellers loitering policemen pastel artists

a unicyclist the statue spray-painted mimes

portrait painters smelly mules a posing vampire

Tour groups were everywhere, moving across the square like schools of fish. Over on Decatur, street acrobats performed to music at the levee-step theater or whatever the thing was called. The dancers had a nice-sized crowd taking in their leapfrogs, cartwheels, moonwalks, prolonged handstands. Spectators oohed, ahhed, clapped, cheered. Parents looked at their children and smiled. I watched and waited for the accident, which, sure enough, happened when a steamboat's horn overtook the music coming from their boom box. When the muffly blare sounded out, a leaping toe clipped a crouching shoulder, and the man lost form, flailed, did a belly flop onto the concrete. Everyone gasped. He was down for a moment, but, of course, got up unassisted, checked his ribs, readjusted his headband, gave a salute. Wild applause came. I knew he'd done it on purpose. I'd seen these guys fuck up like that before, always when some kind of horn sounded out. They probably drew straws before each show to see who'd do it.

It was hot already. Wet. Too fucking tropical. I looked up at the sun, clutched at my shirt collar, shook it. How could anyone perform in this shit?

Over at the church I saw my new friends talking to some people. A few of them were watching me.

-

Last night, after spending Genia's twenty on heatlamp pizza and big lagers I headed to the river rocks, where I tried to sleep amidst the roaches and driftwood and other nasty tide-wrack. It was a rough night. Squalorous, pungent, miserable. Enough to crater a man. Close to the water, I found a place with enough open dirt to lay down, but there were still some pebbles and sticks making it impossible to get comfortable.

Deep into the night, two pair of footsteps stopped close by, up on the walkway. I heard the flicking of a lighter, a growly voice, a higher one, both of them unintelligible. At a certain point their conversation paused. The footsteps came closer, and the high voice said the first thing I was able to make out: "God, is he dead?"

"Maybe he washed up at high tide."

I kept cadaver-still, and they left before long. In the morning, though, I felt a nudging in my ribs. I opened my eyes and saw two silhouettes leaning over me. One was much larger than the other, and this hoss-like creature asked me, in a voice that let me know they were the same guys, what happened to me, if I was robbed, if I was "with anyone."

"No, I'm new to town," I said, squinting up at them, shielding my face.

"Yeah?"

"I'm here all by myself."

"Get up," the little one said.

"Get up? Why?"

"Why not?"

"You guys cops?"

They stared at me.

"Come on," he repeated, in his squeaky voice.

"Fine." I started to find my feet. What else was I going to do? There were two of them after all, and one looked like he had enough blubber to light up a city block's worth of lamps.

When I stood up, the beluga said "Look!" and pointed to my ass. The little one went behind me, and soon they both were giggling epileptically, and doing that thing where people prolong their laughter so you have to acknowledge you're the butt of a joke.

I turned and saw what had them all worked up.

The stain was external, I tried to convince them, which did nothing to quell the laughing. Great. Another thing to add to the list. What had I slept on? I tried to wipe it off on a rock, which didn't work and which made them laugh even more. I guess it didn't matter. I was beat-up, hungover, broke, sore all through my body. There were bigger problems right now. Still though. We were in a high profile region, and now I had this to think about.

"Come on sleeping beauty," the little guy said, "let's go."

Without even asking what they wanted I went along with them across the train tracks, up and over the levee, past the theater, across Decatur, past the smelly mules, and into the square. They told me to sit on a bench and wait.

Here they came, with their friends hanging back, watching. I didn't know if they'd been waiting for me to wake up from my bench nap. Probably not. In their slow approach, they were like an oncoming storm. Twin hurricanes. I decided to call them Danny and Flossy. Flossy, the porkulus, unsurprisingly had some wobble and loll to his stride. They kept bumping into each other, each glancing at the other whenever it happened. When they got closer I saw that Danny, the skinny one, had a bottle of beer, and Flossy had a block of cheese that'd been mutilated by bite-marks.

"Jesus," I said to him, "that's pretty gross."

They estimated me a moment.

"Where do you think he's from?" Danny said in his high-pitched voice, talking to Flossy but looking at me.

"Who cares, man."

"Who *cares*?"

The twerp glanced sharp at the manatee, who flinched a little, looked away.

I looked down at the pavement.

"Hey, Corky, get up," Danny said.

"Huh?" I lifted my head.

"We've been talking about you."

"To who?"

"We have a present."

"We? What present? What do you mean, Corky?"

"Come on."

I glanced over at their friends.

"Look man," I said, "I don't know who you are, what your game is over there. Honestly."

"Come on, Corky. Be a sport. Don't make me keep asking."

I looked over at Flossy, who took a bite of cheese, chewed, stared at me with wide eyes.

A tour group stood by the big statue. As we passed it I picked up part of the guide's lecture, something about the rarity of a rearing horse for the time of production. Most in the group were fat, pasty, elderly. Some looked at us with that recoiling-in-distaste expression the old couple had given me. Danny, oblivious to them and resuming, I guess, a delayed conversation, looked at Flossy and said, "What I don't understand is how you're so much fatter than me. Either I've got the metabolism of a tree shredder or you're sneaking snacks behind my back."

"Well, I don't know what to tell you," Flossy said. "I don't eat any more than you."

"Sure you do. What else could it be?"

Flossy didn't answer.

I looked them over. The two of them were such a micro-cosm of the city's low grade one-upsmanship—when someone had even a tiny advantage over another, denigration was sure to consecrate it.

In the cathedral's tall shadow we came upon the group they'd been talking to, scruffy, gaunt-looking urchins with oily faces and never-changed clothes. I'd seen these types around, the castaways, the down-and-outs, the don't-come-homes. Apparently they'd formed a congregation. They had an interest in me, that was clear. I'd been recruited for something. But what?

One of them, a squat fire hydrant of a man with a ruddy red face, looked at me and shouted "Corky!" The other miscreants smiled at this.

Flossy went up to this guy and whispered something into his ear. The guy looked down, nodded. When Flossy was finished and off to the side the guy came closer to me, and the group started forming a circle around us. I glanced back and forth at them, taking in their grotesquery. Then the pug man said, in a voice that sounded coarsened by years of smoking, "This is Corky. He of the rancid river rocks. The man with the funky trousers. City sludge personified."

Laughter.

Some in the group were looking at the small of his back. I saw he had his hands there, and was making sure to face me directly.

"Corky says he sat on something," he went on, "but we wonder if that's true. Does he say so to save face? Well, I'll tell you what. Whether or not he is, well, that chocolate bullseye makes him lower than the basement beneath Lucifer's boiler room. And we would know. Wouldn't we?"

More laughter.

"Corky," he said. "My friend. *Our* friend." He came closer. I could smell alcohol. "Whoever you are," he said, "and wherever you're from, to you, Corky, Monsieur Fecalpants, we bequeath *this*."

He stepped back, and displayed above his head the thing he'd been hiding: a wreath made of corks and some other lumpy shit that I couldn't quite make out.

The group laughed again, applauded.

"Here is a symbol of our judgement," he said, bringing it back down. "And also, might I add, an effective means of limiting future stain damage."

He stuck the wreath in my face. The thing smelled like a dumpster during a garbagemen's strike. Revolting fumes. Twigs and branches, and wrappers, were mixed in with all the corks. God knows what was making for an adhesive.

He tried to put the thing on my head, and I realized it was a crown, not a wreath. I stepped away from him and he laughed and tried again. This time I knocked the thing out of his hands, and it hit the ground and broke apart.

We all spent a quiet moment staring at the wreckage. Among the shrapnel I saw what might have been peanut butter, old cheese, gum, tape.

"Fine," he said. "Blaspheme if you will. Your fate's the same, regardless!"

He picked up a clump of the broken crown and threw it at me. It hit me in the chest and splattered like a septic snowball. I looked down—another stain to show off.

The disciples laughed, and rushed over and picked up more pieces. They started pelting me with the nasty clumps, sending them whizzing by at warp speed.

"Secular retribution for Judas Christ!" one said.

I ran toward the gate, and went back into the square, passing the tour group that still was at the fountain. Long speech I guess. As I went by, the clumps started hitting them too, almost like they became a preferred target. The victims groaned, assumed defensive postures, hunched. Even a little girl took a dose and started crying after a moment of shock, like when they drop ice cream.

Then the pelts stopped coming.

Out of ammo I guess? Was nailing the kid too much?

I turned and saw them walking away, laughing, heading back to whatever crevice they'd come from.

People in the group were examining themselves. A lot of their fabric was smudged up. Several kneeled by the girl. Some glared at me, like it was my fault. I extended my hands and made a little curtsy, and smiled. No one laughed.

I was safe now, I guess. So then. Where to now? I had no money, and no tangible avenues to pursue. This is what Genia wanted of course—to see me reduced this way. She could never know how much she'd got what she wanted. Jesus, look at me.

Behind me I heard a calliope. A pennywhistle. A trombone, way far off.

Little kids walked by with their parents, faces painted, balloons tied to their wrists. One was skipping which made the parents laugh.

On the St. Peter side of the square, some cops stood in the shade of the big trees. Staring at me. Two of them, each male, each bordering on unprofessionally obese.

They started coming forward.

I got back to walking. Waited for a shouting voice. But it didn't come. I looked over my shoulder and saw them heading in another direction. Something else had snared their attention: an old man from the unlucky tour group, hunched over and furrow-browed, rinsing his shirt in the fountain by the front gate. What the hell was he thinking?

When the officers got close, one said, "Hey there."

The man looked up, went back to his business, no change in his expression. "What?" he said.

"What? Whutchuh *mean*, what?"

The officer grabbed him by the arm and pulled him up. His partner took the other arm, and they started him away from the fountain and the group. In their wake, a lady I assumed was the wife followed at a distance.

As they walked him along, the guy raised his voice, and tried to break away from them. That, I knew right away, was a doomed idea. Sure enough, the cops picked up their pace, and walked him over to the fence that surrounded the statue. They pushed him against it, hard, and pulled out his wallet. While one checked the ID, the other handcuffed him. The first guy took out a walkie talkie. The wife came up and tried to speak to the officers, but only got an extended palm and a standoffish "Ma'am."

This is where I caught a break, actually several, when you factor in all the people who had to have missed it: the cop returned the wallet to the guy's pocket carelessly, and as they turned him back around, it fell out of his pocket, through the fence, and into a bush. No one else witnessed this—not the cops, not the man, not the gawking tour group, not any random lookie loos. Not even the wife. No one but me.

They took him all the way to Decatur, with the wife following, and ducked him into a squad car that had pulled up by the carriages. Or was it there already? Whatever the case, they got inside and the car took off instantly. When they'd gone the wife stood there for a second, before taking a phone out of her fanny pack and walking hurriedly up Decatur.

I turned back to see how the tour group had received this, but they were gone. The guide knew to hustle them out of there I guess. Why didn't he tell the old man to stay the hell away from the fountain?

I looked back at the bush. This seemed like such improbable good fortune. I wondered if it was an inside job, if another officer would come by and scoop it up. Then I wondered if some lucky jackass would stumble upon it while I stood here pontificating.

After looking out for witnesses, I crouched. Reached between the bars. Felt the warm leather. Put it in my pocket.

Walking away, I got a strange feeling that someone had seen me. That someone would call out, start running. At the St. Anne exit, I imagined getting tackled from behind, or attacked by dogs, lassoed, tasered, blow-darted. I swiveled and scanned for pursuers, forgetting the small steps right before the exit. Three strides into my swooping pan, I stumbled into a bush.

3.

Along black space, punctured by discomfort: I was beneath a fallen tree. Swallowed by ivy. Buried in foliage?

It was dark. Crisp air and wet-smelling pavement signaled the outside.

What else? My ribs hurt. Head. I'd been struck.

They'd left me. They wouldn't come back.

Was that what I wanted to believe?

I tried to get to my feet, but couldn't. I was muddled up. Weighed down. Dizzy. I'd been drinking, but my sense of things seemed too convoluted, my skull too throbbing with pain, my body too immobile, to blame everything on alcohol.

Off in the distance a voice called out. No response came.

Birds chirped.

When I got a little more sorted I saw I was covered with giant tree branches. Blanketed by them in fact.

I clawed my way out, stood up. Too fast. God, will I vomit?

I was in an alley: barbwired fences, drooping phone lines, copper lamplight.

More branches were in a nearby dumpster. Actually, they were scattered all over the place.

My head stung. I reached up and touched it, pulled my hand back, saw red fingertips.

Would I need stitches?

With my eyes out for any living thing I walked down the alley, turned left, got onto Prytania. A pool of deep ochre started to spill over the sky. More birds chirped.

4.

Wincing from a new collage of scrapes on my face, hands, and forearms, I surged forth with my prize, bumping tourists and slaloming around them. They didn't find me funny—many frowned and gave prissy, disapproving looks. A beefy dude with his twinkly lady friend glared like he'd come after me.

By the time I hit Decatur I was out of breath. Had to slow down. As I did a police car went by, sirens on and blaring. Was that for me? Seemed unlikely. Squad cars don't tear down the street for a wallet. But then I saw it stop at the square.

On the first corner I saw a series of giant ferns hanging from the huge, hooked-open windows of a Creole restaurant. Everyone inside the restaurant looked busy: diners enraptured by their heart attack cuisine, servers whisking about balancing trays, fetching bills, clearing tables. Down the block, a brown fence began near the last open window. About halfway down the fence I saw a slight opening. A gate.

—

A tight, back-of-the-house area was marked off by

blurry windows   big black barrels   an awning

blurry windows   plastic chairs and a table
                                      (beneath the awning)

a back door   trash bins

Three tall brick buildings in claustrophobic proximity to one another were covered by veins of ivy and patches of black moss. Balconies with ferns and flowerpots decorated the one to the right. Every window had closed blinds or drawn curtains.

A heap of kitchen floor mats had been piled by the restaurant's back door. A steam gun connected to a hose lay on top of them. Looking through the door, I saw two servers, way far down, backs to me, standing at a welcome podium. The front door was a bright gleam of light that obscured them, made them shadows.

Over to the right, silhouettes moved in the blurry windows.

I heard clanging metal, water running through pipes, smelled burning pork that mingled with a type of smoke I knew all too well.

This was creepy. Too high profile, too much in hiding.

I went and grabbed hold of the gate. Before I opened it,

though, a rustling came from behind me. I looked back, and saw a gangly man, accompanied by a cloud of smoke, come up from behind the barrels. He was surprised to see me.

"Who are you?" he said.

I laughed, smelling the smoke, knowing right away what had him talking sharp. "Now, how in the hell do you think you're gonna get away with *that*?" I said.

He came out from behind the barrels and moved toward me with an expression that reminded me of the last time I saw Genia.

"What are you doing in here?"

A damp white shirt and nametag suggested a server at the end of his shift. He had a nice watch, a necklace. His arms were all inked up with tattoos. I read his nametag: KEVIN.

I looked at the steam gun. Genia once told me mat spraying was the worst sidework a server can have, the worst card to draw. This guy was probably smoking to anesthetize himself for one more push after a hard morning on the floor.

"Are you here for someone?" he said.

"Uh," I looked into the restaurant, "is Jen here?"

"*Jen*?"

"Yeah, Jen."

He shook his head, inhaled through his nose. "No," he said. "I don't think Jen's here."

"Ah."

I put my hands in my pockets—when I did this, he looked down at them.

"You're dirty," he said.

"Yeah."

"Kind of beat up."

"Yeah."

"Are you in trouble?"

"I'm not sure, Kevin."

"Well," he said. "What do you need here?"

"Lots of stuff. I'm hungry, thirsty, sober, and dirty. Is this, by any chance, a good place to remedy those maladies?"

He looked confused.

"Do what now?"

"I mean, like, get a drink maybe."

He stared at me. Then tilted his head at the mats. "I have to clean those," he said.

"Oh," I looked at them, nodded.

His confused look returned. Without saying anything, he went inside. At that point, leaving would probably have been the smart thing to do, but something told me I needed to get a thing or two going here, to generate momentum, find my sea legs, burn clouds away. It made me feel better to think I was on the upswing. But I needed some proof that I was.

I faced away from where he'd gone in, pulled out the

wallet, and saw an encouraging slab of green. Before I could get into it though, footsteps came up behind me. I turned around and saw Kevin with his hands on his hips, squinting, smiling a little.

"You really want a drink?" he said.

"Well," I said, putting the wallet away. "Maybe."

He nodded.

"Give me a minute," he said. "Okay?"

He worked with concentration, blasting the rubber at close range, flipping it, blasting it some more. The mist from the gun made the area even more damp and humid. As he worked he'd glance over at me and smile, give a quick nod. I'd nod back. When finally he finished and had taken some of the mats back into the restaurant, I went through the wallet. Inside was just over $400 cash, most of it fifties and twenties, along with credit cards, a tracking card from Harrah's Casino, a rotary club membership, a driver's license. Jacob Schmidt, from Carson City, Nevada. 57 years old. I took the bills and distributed them in my shirt and pants pockets and committed to memory how much I had where. When I was about done repeating the numbers to myself, Kevin came back into the doorway.

He lit a cigarette, took a drag, estimated me.

"You've done something, boy," he said. "Haven't you?"

"Kevin," I said looking at his exhale. "Let me ask you a question."

"Yeah?"

"For twenty dollars, would you give me a hose shower?"

"A what?"

"Not with that gun though. With the regular hose."

"Huh," he said. "A shower."

"I need to get cleaned up. Badly."

He took another drag. "Someone put their claws on you," he said, "didn't they?"

Before I could answer he went back inside and returned almost immediately with three guys dressed in baggy white T-shirts and checkered pants. They stood in the doorway staring at me along with Kevin. One of them came forward, a scrawny, bony-faced man with sharp cheekbones whose diminutive stature made for a sharp contrast to the other two.

"He wanna what?" this guy said. "A hose *shower*?"

No one responded. I needed to get out of here, I thought. Maybe start running now.

He came closer to me, pulled up about a slap's reach away. "How'd you get in here?" he said, looking over at the gate. "Shit. Hose shower. We ought to tell Carla. Or Trish! That's what *I'd* do. *Hose shower.*"

"I need one, is the thing. I can't do it myself."

He stared at me a second, started back toward the others, half-turned, and said, "That's what you're looking for?

A goddamn hose shower?"

I reached into my left shirt pocket and grabbed a twenty. "Actually," I said, holding the money out, "I kind of hoped I could get some lunch too."

He looked at the money, up at me, and started yelling about who the fuck was *I*, did I know hard it was to be a cook, working until two in the morning sometimes, waiters on your ass, management too? He was jabbing fingers at the air, looking me up and down, leaning forward and wobbling his head. Not long into this tirade, Kevin, maybe seeing he'd made a mistake, tried to intervene; "Come on, now," he said, touching the guy's shoulder. But the guy shook Kevin off.

"Who the fuck are you, coming in throwing money around?" he said. "Who'd you take it from, huh? I know you didn't make that."

He got as close to me as Ruddy Face did in the square, but unlike Ruddy Face, he got quiet, like it was my turn to say something. The dude was crazy—I had no idea how to placate him. How could I show him deference on the turf I'd invaded?

I remembered something Genia told me about cooks in New Orleans. "Um," I said, "can you sell me four nickel bags by any chance?"

He stepped back, looked over at his friends. They smiled.

"Oh you like a little bit of that fire?"

I held out the twenty.

While I smoked a cigarette Kevin sat beneath the awning, breaking up the weed. I stared at the cigarette's white filter, and the growing brown blur inside it. I felt shaken by what'd happened. A lot of relationships started on strange and volatile terms down here, but angry, pot-selling cooks who knew about my bankroll seemed like something that'd cause problems, not solve them.

"You like these minty menthols?" I said, still looking at the filter.

Kevin laughed. "Don't worry about him," he said.

That was no kind of answer to my question.

In the small blurry windows, shadows moved about. Sounds of clanking dishes could be heard. Kevin eyed me watching them for a moment, then stood and said, "Ready?"

He was holding the joint out at me.

"Let's wait," I said, stamping my cigarette out.

"Yeah?"

"Actually, you can have that."

"Oh yeah?" he said. "What are you gonna do with the rest?"

"Yours."

"Well, how about that!" he said, pocketing everything. "Let's put an order in. You're hungry, right?"

"Do I have to go inside?"

"No," he said. "We'll get Lily out here. She'll put you on

my number before I sign out."

"Sounds good."

Now he was my buddy. I considered his acquiescence. He didn't ask me why I wanted what I wanted. That was always a red flag. Also, he didn't thank me for the weed.

Sounds of a marching band arose. Drumbeats, percussion, horns. Very quickly the noises grew louder. A hail of music came over us: rapid drumming, blunt tuba blasts, the trumpet wailing so rooted in the city. It got so loud it was like they were in the courtyard with us. Kevin stared at the fence as if he could see through it. When the music began to fade he turned to me, with a huge, sociable grin on his face. That was a New Orleans trick, to parlay an upbeat feeling into lucrative congeniality. Like most outsiders with money, I'd play along, because there was something in it for me too.

I reached into my pocket. As before, his eyes went down to my hands. "You know," he said, "we've got cake with caramel icing, one inch thick." He held his thumb and finger up to show. "You want some?"

"I may need to get soap first," I said, "so I can wash up."

"We can get soap."

"But do you think I could see a menu?"

"A menu? Sure!" He leaned forward and called into the back door, "Hey! Get Lily!"

No one replied, but in a minute a female server came out, a young, pale girl who looked pissed off. Loose strands of hair were sticking to her sweaty face. She was frowning, slumping her shoulders a little. When she got closer I saw her nametag was a piece of cardboard safety-pinned to her shirt. LILY had been scrawled on the cardboard with a thick black marker.

"Why are you yelling for me?"

"Can you add a one top?" Kevin said.

"Huh?"

"Use the special code. Table 922."

"You want me to take one more?" she lifted her chin and grimaced to her molars. "I'm handling three tables inside, and I should be off the clock."

"I'm a good tipper," I said, smiling.

She looked at me.

"Go talk to Carla if you have if you have a problem," Kevin said. "Just get some water, and-"

He turned to me.

I looked at Kevin, the girl, back at Kevin.

"A Coke and an Abita?"

"There you go," he said. "A Coke and an Abita. Chop chop youngster! And bring out some bread."

"Out here? Bring it out here?"

"What'd I just say?"

She shook her head and turned around, whooshing her ponytail.

He looked at me, smiled, winked.

"Got another cigarette?" I said.

"Sure do."

He lit me up.

Members of the morning crew started to leave through the back gate. Most were in good moods, it seemed, talking, laughing, in no apparent hurry to be someplace. They all waved at Kevin. Some even nodded at me, though most regarded me as a confusing entity. I had yet to see new workers enter. Did they come in through the front when they were clean and fresh-looking?

Lily came back out with my beer only.

"Thank you," I said.

"I'm not supposed to be handling tables by myself," she said to Kevin. "Technically, I'm still being trained. The customers are getting mad at me too. I keep messing up, and coming out here slows me down. We really have to serve him out here?"

"Ah, Jesus," Kevin said.

"And you won't give me any share of the tips. That's wrong. Even if I'm a trainee, you're supposed to tip me out. Even if I'm only assisting you. And I'm doing more than assisting, I'm covering for you."

"Jeeessssuuuuus!" he turned to me. "Acting like she's a trainee. How can she know something like that if she's just a trainee?"

"She's been around."

She turned to me.

"Been around?"

"Sorry," I said. "You know what I mean."

Kevin laughed.

When she went back inside, he winked at me again, and got up and ducked behind the barrels. I leaned back in my chair and looked up at the sky, where marshmallowey clouds hovered above the rooftops.

Lily took my order: crawfish etouffee and another Abita. When she'd gone back inside, after speaking to me with what I considered somewhat unfriendly economy, I turned to the barrels.

"How's it going over there?"

A thumbs-up appeared.

"Want some?"

"Nah."

She put two plates, one big and one small, next to the bread basket, on a chair I'd made into a table.

"So why are we serving you outside?" she said.

"Do you really want me inside?"

She didn't answer.

"I paid extra for this," I said. "Because I know it's extra work for you."

"Who are you?" she said, brushing her hair behind her ear.

"Where'd I come from?"

"Yeah."

"I came from the I-10."

"The what?"

"I'm a musician, you see, and I've been separated from my group."

"Where's your group?"

"Right now, Canal, probably. The Sheraton."

"You don't have a phone?"

I shook my head. "Don't remember their numbers, either," I said.

"What happened?"

A rustling came from behind the barrels. Up popped Kevin. "You're a musician?" he said.

"Yup."

"You playing somewhere tonight?"

"Uh, the Maple Leaf," I said. "Uptown."

Lily's eyes grew. "Oh my God," she said, "are you part of the DJ Revolution show?"

I smirked.

"Oh, hell yeah."

"Awesome!"

She held still and focused on me. Her head tilted a little.

"So do you have a name?" she said.

I didn't know if she meant my DJ name.

5.

Saturated by the wet morning air, I walked past half-circle driveways, shuttered storefronts, puddles, giant oaks. I realized that to get out of this rut I had to look for better patterns and make them interior. But first, what to tell Genia? Actually, first, block out observers. That wasn't easy—no matter how hard I tried I kept seeing my reflection, if not in a window than in someone's body language.

Finally, I hit a stretch with no pedestrians. Few cars. Okay.

For starters, Andrew was the only player I knew. Why didn't I try to keep him around? Did I have a say? If he didn't bust so early he'd have stayed, and the whole thing might never have happened. I should have left with him. Maybe not. Anyway, what was he supposed to do, wait all night for me to finish because I couldn't handle myself in a roomful of strangers?

I was all over the place.

They got me drunk. I remembered that. Shot after shot they'd set up for me, and I kept putting them down.

-

All along the avenue mansions and beat-up apartments occupied the same blocks. St. Charles had a reputation for luxury, but anyone who'd spent time here knew the truth: wealth and destitution cohabited.

Atop the steps of a coffee shop, a skinny little man dressed in a windbreaker and black jeans looked out at the street. Cradling a stack of newspapers. When he saw me, he nodded and smiled. "Almost open!" he said, thumbing over his shoulder.

I stopped, forgetting that in New Orleans, you never stop.

"Hey," he said, with a look of concern. "Are ya al*right*? You're looking kind of straggly."

"Uh, yeah, I'm okay," I said, touching the back of my head, although I wasn't hurt there.

"Oh okay. Want a newspaper?"

I looked at them, shook my head.

He nodded, reached into his shirt pocket, and took out a cigarette.

"Got a light?"

"No," I said, "I don't."

"Alright."

He put the cigarette back.

"Ya seem like you're in bad shape," he said.

"You know," I said, taking a step away from him, "I've got nothing on me. Literally."

He paused a moment.

"Well," he said, "I just want ya to know, I'm a homeless man, alright, and I sell newspapers. Alright?"

"Yeah?"

"Most of the homeless," he said, "they're lazy, ya see, they're not out doing *nothin*. Especially at this time of day. They don't wanna do nothin but beg, alright, and just *sit around*. Just *lazy*. It's like they-"

"Gave up?"

He laughed. "Man, I could tell you some stories. *Real bad ones*."

"Well," I said, "you seem to have come through better than most."

"Hey, do you mind if I walk with ya to that restaurant over there?" he pointed down the street, to where I saw only houses. "I need to use the restroom."

"Um. Sure."

-

A black truck stopped in the middle of the embankment and waited to make a left turn. This halted the progress of an uptown-bound streetcar. The car's passengers—undoubtedly tourists—looked out at the scenery with smiles on their faces, as if they were on an amusement park ride. Some took pictures. Stoppages like these always got worse reactions from downtown-bound cars filled with city workers.

In one of the seats, an old man stared into the sun. No sunglasses, no squinting—just a solemn, stone-faced look. His head stayed in that same position, expression unchanged, even when the car got rolling again.

I turned to my new friend. Saw him staring at me.

"Long day ahead," he said.

"Always."

"What do you got goin on?"

"Personal matters, mostly."

"Oh, alright."

"How about you?"

"I'll be out making friends," he said.

I smiled.

"Do ya believe," he said, "I've been offered work by people out here, just from comin up to them and telling them my story?"

I stopped.

"Oh yeah?"

"Oh yeah!"

He smiled.

"I think we're going around in circles," I said

"Huh?"

"Look."

I turned my pockets inside out.

"I tell my girl I'm in real estate."

He looked up at me, repositioned himself, smiled, exhaled, glanced away, shook his head, and went back to his little stoop, muttering, walking with the body language of an overslacked string puppet.

6.

Woozily satisfied from a buttery, oversalted and lard-enhanced entrée, I leaned back in my chair and watched clouds snail past the rooftops. I thought about my presence here. In this improvisation, a quick wallet check had turned into a drug hookup I didn't want, mild flirtation with a waitress, carte blanche status in a fancy restaurant's backyard, the evolution of a new identity perhaps. On that note, I'd given Kevin money to get me a few things from the store. We even made a list together. Before heading out he'd gone back behind the barrels again, to celebrate his good fortune, I suppose.

"Need anything?" Lily said, as she cleared the last of the dishes.

I looked back down.

"Nope. I'm good."

"Really? Another drink maybe?"

"Well, okay."

"No problem," she smiled.

"Thank you."

She nodded at my shirt.

"You're missing some buttons. You know that?"

"Yeah."

"What happened?"

"Lost them in a poker game."

She smiled again, crinkling her nose this time. Watching her walk away, I thought about the rules she inspired me to remember: be easy to talk to, get into an environment where you'll see them more than once, carry an egoless conversation, end it on good terms. The next time you meet, you'll know in the first ten seconds what kind of girl she is and how she feels about you. If it's no good, you move on, or pay for a lack of pride.

—

"Who are your influences?" she said.

"Lots of the local guys."

"Local guys? Like who?"

"Juvee, for one."

"Oh really?"

"That's right."

"Who else?"

"Are you done?" said Kevin, who was fresh off his smoke session, not yet running my errand, sitting next to me with a Miller Lite I'd bought him. He was talking to Lily, wearing an expression that reminded me of our first exchange.

"Done with what?" Lily said.

"Don't you have other tables?"

"Wrapped up," she said. "And I made a deal to roll everyone's silver for my sidework."

"So roll it, then."

"I have to wait on him first."

"Unnh."

"Maybe I can bring the silver out here," she said.

"You can't roll silver outside. Are you crazy?"

She dropped her jaw and stared over at me.

"Hey," I said, "if it were up to me, you could bring out drinks for all of us-"

"Well-"

Kevin waved his finger and shook his head. "No, finish up here. Hurry up."

I felt like maybe he was talking to both of us. What was his problem?

Lily started for the door. Before she disappeared inside, though, Kevin said, "Hey there."

She turned.

"What?"

"Wanna make a little cash?"

"What?"

"Can you go to Walgreen's?"

"Why would I do that?" she said.

"We need to get our friend a few things. For his shower."

"His shower?" she looked at me.

"We'll make it worth your while," he said. "You can roll the silver later."

Kevin held up some money and the list, and Lily came back and held still while he put everything in her apron pocket. This transaction was broached and completed in the blink of an eye. No misunderstandings. No follow up questions. And she didn't seem too preoccupied with the strangeness of the request. I was confused by that, and by why Kevin would give up money I'd given him. Maybe he saw it as low-status to carry out my bidding, although I'm sure for the right price I could have insisted he go. Was he testing to see if I'd do that? And how did the two of them have such a tight line of communication all of a sudden?

"She's from Gretna," he said to me in a confidential tone as we watched her leave. "Three kids already."

"Yeah?"

Three kids. That was hard to believe. She seemed too petite, too young, although when you stared real hard you could see tattoos through her sweat-dampened shirt: a circular design on the left shoulder blade, something big across the small of her back.

We sat in silence for a moment.

"Sure you don't wanna smoke?" he said.

I looked over and saw him grinning, raised eyebrows, narrowed eyes.

"No, I'm okay," I said.

"Is it the quality of the stuff?"

"No."

"Because I've got some friends that sell better stuff. Other things too. Whatever you want. We could meet you somewhere."

I nodded. He stared at me a second, then finished his

beer, got up, and went inside. Watching him go, I thought again about how I probably needed to leave this place. But I was enjoying myself, and still had to take my shower. And where the fuck would I go anyway? Back to Genia in defeat?

Lily came out and walked over to the gate. "See you soon," she said, smiling and giving me a wiggling-fingers wave. I waved back.

After she left I sat there awhile without any company. At one point I looked up, and saw, in one of the windows above the restaurant, a woman staring down at me. She wore all black, and stood in front of a black background. She looked like she was staring down at a coffin. I brought my head down fast.

A sharp female voice arose inside the restaurant. I didn't catch the words, except "*sayin?*" Then shouting. Profanities. Lots of voices. It kept on, until one voice seemed to snuff out the rest, the same female one from before, saying "No. *No.*" Soon thereafter a tall, wide-torsoed woman in khaki shorts and a blue shirt came outside. Angry-looking. When she saw me, she walked straight over, with Kevin following close behind. A few people had come to the doorway and they stayed there and watched.

She had a broad, square face pocked with moles. Frizzy hair. Some words were tattooed across the inside of her left forearm. When she got closer I saw her nametag: CARLA.

"Who are you?" she said.

"Um," I looked at Kevin, who only shrugged, "I'm some

guy off the street."

"Miss Trish says there's too much noise down here."

"I told you," Kevin said. "We'll be quiet."

"No, you won't."

I'd pushed my luck too far. My need to feel on top of things and my self-serving optimism had done me in again. I began to think about waiting on the sidewalk for Lily and forgetting about the shower, or just taking off altogether.

"Who is this?" Carla said, keeping her eyes on me.

Kevin didn't answer.

"Carla," I said, standing up, dropping the cigarette and stamping it out, "I've been out here running people around. I ought to know better. I'm sorry."

She crossed her arms, leaned forward, and made like she was smelling me. "Boy," she said, "you been at the trough too long."

"Yes, well, I'm taking a shower-"

"You can't be out here like this," she said. "Trish is comin' down soon."

I didn't respond.

She kept staring at me—as with the cooks, I interpreted the silence as my cue to speak.

"Carla," I put my hands in my pockets. "I know the time of your staff is valuable, that I've been wasting it, and that *you're* at the top of the pyramid. I do know that."

Her eyes followed my hands, but she didn't look right back up the way Kevin did.

"Listen," I said. "I need someone to do me a favor."

She looked at me.

"What's that, piggy?"

"I need someone to go to Cotton Market on St. Phillip-"

"I know Cotton Market."

"Get me a pair of khakis, two cotton shirts and some socks."

"Why?"

"I just need clothes. There's a $50 tip, and you can keep the change."

"Yeah?"

I pulled out $150, and offered it to her. She looked at it unhappily. "I don't need that money," she said. "And why the hell would you even ask someone to do that?"

"There and back. Easy right? Can you guess my size?"

She looked at Kevin. "I'll do it," he said.

"No."

I pulled out $50 more.

"I really need a break here, Carla."

"You must be some kind of goddamned idiot," she said.

"I hope you're only half right."

She took the money at that amount.

Before opening the gate she turned and glanced at the windows above the restaurant. When she opened the gate, Lily was standing there, just about to knock I guess, with shopping bags in her hand. Holy shit she was fast! Had she found everything?

Carla spoke to her, too quietly for me to hear, then turned and squinted at me, and, frowning, took the bags from Lily, dropped them inside the area, walked out onto the sidewalk, and shut the gate.

Rustling through the bags I saw Lily had found everything, even gray dye, which I thought would be a longshot. Change and the receipt were included. What an honest girl. I felt a little depressed she was gone though, and that she hadn't scribbled her number down somewhere for me. Didn't she have to clock out, roll silver, enter information into the house log? Say goodbye? I didn't understand how she could just disappear even if an agitated Carla had said just get on out of here, but then again, as far as my core interests were concerned, it was a nonissue. The situation had been managed enough for me to get a shower, get a change of clothes, split, and worry about all the rest later. I just needed Carla to hurry the hell back.

I turned to Kevin.

"I think it's time for my shower."

"You still want to do that?"

"I paid for it didn't I?"

"Okay, but quick. And when Carla comes back, you get dressed and go."

I removed the shampoo, soap, and towel from the shopping bags, took off my shirt, and walked to the center of the courtyard. The crowd that'd come out to see Carla was still by the door, and most were smiling now.

When I was ready to go, I turned and nodded.

"We're doing this fast," he said.

He started spraying me. I lathered up and scrubbed, and soon, glaciers of dirt were sliding off my body and dried blood was coming out of my hair. "Keep going," I said. "Keep going. More."

Voices arose by the back door. Giggles.

"Woo wee," someone said, "don't miss any spots!"

"Look at all that slop!"

Kevin put his thumb on the mouth of the hose and sprayed me harder. Their laughter rose, and even he was laughing. He sprayed me like that for some time and then everyone got quiet, and fast, as if all the excitement was driven full-speed into a brick wall. I opened my eyes and saw, standing with everyone else at the door, the lady from the window. She was heavily made-up, short, doughy-in-stature, wearing a black dress that was so tight her body looked like a squeezed water balloon.

She smiled at me. "Hello, soldier," she said. "Are you keeping my staff entertained?"

"Well, not on purpose," I said, smoothing my hair back.

"Afraid to take off your pants?"

I looked down.

"I suppose I am."

"If I were you, I'd be afraid to keep them on."

"You might be right, ma'am."

She turned to Kevin, and said, "Well what are ya waitin for?"

He started spraying me again, with Water Balloon instructing him where to douse me, and laughing. But everyone else had became eerily quiet. All I could hear was her cackling voice and the water hitting me, splattering on the ground. This went on until the gate door clicked, and Kevin let up the hose and we all looked over to see Carla standing there with a plastic bag in one hand and a box of wine in the other. She looked stunned at what she was witnessing. Damn, I thought. As fast as Lily. Did I ask for the wine?

Water Balloon put a fist to her hip and said, "And where have *you* been?" She was smiling, but Carla sure as hell wasn't.

Carla stood there, quiet, dumbfounded. I went up to her and took everything with no objection, even the wine, and said, "Thanks."

The staff started going back inside. Seeing their manager humbled was disheartening, I guess. Kevin stayed behind, though, and watched us while coiling the hose as slow as he could.

"Carla," said Water Balloon.

"Ma'am."

"Go see that everything's alright inside."

"Yes ma'am."

Carla disappeared.

I began toweling off.

Water Balloon looked over at me. "How long have you been out here?" she said. "Did someone serve you?"

"I had a drink," I said. "And a meal. I also paid for that hose-down."

"Were you smoking pot?"

"No ma'am."

"Was anyone?"

"I couldn't say."

She gave a little laugh.

"Are you trying to hustle my staff?" she said.

"No, ma'am."

"Because that's the same thing as trying to outhustle me."

"Yes ma'am."

She looked me up and down. I smelled alcohol, perfume, and the stench of her cosmetics. So much makeup was caked onto her face I wondered how long she could stay out here before it all started melting.

"What are you after?" she said.

"After?" I said. "Ma'am, I am in the middle of a rocky gambling binge. To tell you the truth, I wanted to have a private meal in peace, out in the sun. So I paid extra for it."

"Is that right?"

"And I felt like getting cleaned up, and everyone here's just been so nice-"

She laughed.

"Well, that's wonderful!"

"I know."

"So what's with the cuts and bumps? Did you get beat up?"

"A little bit, ma'am. But not by anyone from your staff."

She looked down at the wine.

"You're not entirely cleaned up, you know," she said.

"I know."

"Why don't you come use my bathroom?" she said. "You can bring all your things with you."

"Really?"

Without saying anything else, she walked over to the barrels Kevin had been hiding behind. I followed, and saw that just around the corner was a twisting staircase.

At the first step I turned back around and looked at the tiny little area I'd been in. In the middle of it was Kevin's long shadow, still coiling the hose.

7.

A jet boated through the sky and left a wake of rumbling thunder sounds. Just above the treetops, pelicans passed. At my feet, leaves, bark flakes and branches covered cracked sidewalk.

Jean shorts and baggy T-shirts concealed too much. Shady kids. One went by, and another. Rarely did you see them in groups. With each, it was a similar thing:

"How ya doin partner?...Whatcha say there!...Say there-"

All around the tracks, little yellow-centered daisies grew from mud in the rail ruts. Girls jogged along, red-faced, sweaty.

Here came one more.

As she passed me, we spied each other. I couldn't help but stop and watch her go. Not far from me, a kid standing by a streetcar stop was doing the same thing. I looked him over: big face, square features, eyebrows that made shadows. He wore a short-sleeve dress shirt. At his feet was a suitcase marked with pecks of exposed cardboard.

He turned and saw me, and gave a little flinch. Then he smiled, looked back at the girl. "I wonder how much it'd cost to take *her* downtown," he said.

We stood there, watching her get smaller.

"Tell her you're in real estate," I said.

"Huh?"

"You have to lie up."

"Lie up?"

"Yeah, you know, your most strategic of bullshit. You either lie up, or lie down."

"I'd like to lie down," he said. "With *her.*"

I began to walk away.

"Hey," he said. "Are you okay?"

I stopped. Laughed.

"God."

8.

A bit light-headed from the quick trip up, I followed Water Balloon through narrow French doors and a dark foyer, into an overchilled front room with light green walls that were decorated by Mardi Gras masks, a giant mirror, bookshelves. Bead necklaces drooped from doorknobs, hung on picture frames, crowned lampshades. At the far right an open fireplace next to a giant television had an iron crate filled with lava rocks. Beneath our feet, a hardwood floor looked so shiny it seemed like you could roll a bowling ball across it; close to a doorway by the kitchen, though, was a deep scratch that reminded me of a finger swipe in cake frosting. She must have been sensitive to this, because just a quick glimpse of it brought contempt out of her. "Oh great," she said. "Even you noticed."

"It's not too bad."

"Yes it is. The idiot floor buffer did that with his contraption. I'm threatening to sue."

"That so?"

"This property is owned by the city," she said, "Not me. I had to let that idiot come in here. Why should *I* pay to fix it?"

"They make you keep the inside up? Do they have inspectors or something?"

"Technically, no," she said, moving behind me, "but I'm

required, off the record, to hold events. Officials want to eat in my restaurant then come up here and mingle on the balcony. In return, I get a small price break."

I heard the door lock.

"How much, if you don't mind me asking?"

She didn't answer. I turned, and saw her standing in the foyer doorway, looking like an expanded version of the portrait I saw in the window: still, dull-faced, legs that looked like they'd snap her high heels.

"I'll tell you what," she said, nodding at the things by my feet. "You can trade me that box of wine for a drink."

"Yeah?"

"You know how hard it is for me to sneak in the cheap shit? I have a reputation to uphold!"

I laughed. "But you brought me up here," I said. "What does that do to your reputation?"

Without answering me, she came over, took the wine, and went into the kitchen.

I stood there in my towel, listening to the air conditioner churn. Shivered a little. Why the hell was I here? Was she was creating jealousy downstairs, putting the workers in their places? Were the cops on their way? Before I could really meditate on it, she was back out with what looked like a Manhattan, which she handed to me, and some soda drink for herself.

"What's that?" I said, looking at hers.

"A wine cooler for the princess bishop."

"What's in it?"

"The same thing that's in all of 'em," she said, showing me up close, "soda and piss wine!"

We sipped. Definitely a Manhattan for me.

I looked around the apartment.

"I've seen you before," she said.

"You have?"

"Why were you handing out money so freely?"

"I'm in a generous mood."

She was quiet.

For a second I felt snared in a trap, until she said, while looking at her drink, "You're just an excuse to get out of a boring conversation."

"Oh," I said. "With who?"

She stared at me, then looked down at my things and said, "Go take your drink into the bathroom and get cleaned up."

"Uh, alright."

"And come out and have another with me, and you can be on your way."

She pointed to a hallway door. I gathered my things and did as she said, not wanting to get into a back-and-forth with her. A quick estimation told me there'd be nothing in it for me but overexposure.

A small window inside the shower, obscured by a skyline of soaps, shampoos, and lotions, gave a view of the courtyard area down below, and Decatur. A man on the sidewalk walked by with a toddler on his shoulders. Two old ladies. A fat couple. Twentysomethings with plastic yards. I waited for someone to look up at me, but no one did.

When I got out I shaved my beard down to a goatee using Mr. Schmidt's ID as a guide, grimacing with every stroke of the cheap razor Lily'd bought. After I was finished I colored my hair and goatee gray with a deluge of instant touch-up.

The khakis Carla bought made a nice fit. The dress shirt was too big. I put it on, tucked it in, and surveyed myself in the mirror. Checking my appearance against the ID, I judged it less than a perfect match, but close enough.

When I came out, Water Balloon, who was reclining on her couch, sat up and tensed a little. Just as fast, she gave a wide-eyed smile. "Hey frostyface," she said. "What's with the getup? Are you selling fried chicken?"

"Decided it was time for a change," I said. "For the better, that is."

"In that shirt? You'll suffocate out there."

"Oh, *really*."

"Want another drink?"

"Of course I do."

She took my empty glass and walked across the besmirched hardwood floor, her heels making sounds like hammer strikes in the cavernous apartment. I took note of the way her flesh wobbled back and forth on her frame. She actually looked more like an hourglass made of Jello than a water balloon. I guessed she was in disguise from a former life, at the top of a hierarchy but not born into it. She didn't wear the luxury well enough to convince me of that. But neither had she risen on her own merit. Someone had given her all this. The situation screamed out rich, patronizing husband, but I didn't detect that presence here. No pictures of a man were anywhere to be seen, just shots of her on Bourbon Street, by the river, some of her at parties dressed in Jelloey evening gowns. How long had the poor bastard been dead, was the question.

She came back and handed me my drink.

"Thanks again."

"Come on," she said, and walked me into a den and over to a sliding glass door at the room's far end. When she opened it, warm air burst upon us like a wave.

We sat in iron chairs and looked out at Decatur, the river, the square. Out on the river boats moved across mud-colored water. Orange clouds lingered in the sky. To the right, the sun sank into a horizon of rooftops and made the Quarter look like it had gone ablaze.

I saw the church, nestled between other architectural antiques. A familiar need came over me: to feel some kind of structure was making sense of things. But I didn't want to think about that.

"What happened to the top of that building?" I said, pointing to construction work on the corner of Chartres and St. Anne.

"The hurricane of 1915 damaged the top, I think," she

said, looking over. "They're just now fixing it."

"I see."

I sipped my drink.

"So," she said. "You're going to some kind of party?"

"Something like that."

She nodded. Sipped her drink. Something seemed to be making her unhappy.

"Do you really want to know why I was in the couryard for so long?"

She looked at me, smiled, looked away, up toward St. Anne. Beneath us, a waitress I didn't recognize came out of the restaurant and walked over to one of the square's iron fences. She reached through the bars and put down something in foil—most likely food for the cats, which would stay in hiding until it was dark and the gates were closed. On her way back in, the waitress smiled at someone.

More silence. It was making me uncomfortable. What was there to say? Didn't she have more questions about my new appearance? My old one?

I looked behind us.

"Not a bad setup you have here, huh?"

She didn't reply.

I turned back to the square.

"What about a girlfriend?" she said. "Is there a Mrs. Frostyface?"

I looked over and saw her peering at me from behind her glass. God, she was as awkward as me. It was surprising.

Did my gutter-dwelling persona excite her?

"I have one, I think," I said.

"You think?"

"We met in June."

"Where?"

"Uptown. I was staying in an apartment, she was working at Superior Grill. You know Superior Grill?"

"Why do you say you think you have a girlfriend?"

"Recently she gave me the boot."

"Why?"

"Well," I said, looking at my drink, and the cherry that'd sunk to the bottom of it, "I suffered a financial setback. A poker buddy dealt himself the Judas card, and it kind of spiraled downward from there."

She was quiet again.

Here we were, settling into a pattern.

"The thing is," I said, "you get fooled. Some girls have a way of making you think you have all kinds of authority, then you get carried away with it."

No reply.

-

"You start judging conversations by the approval of an imagined ally, and soon you're on the road to condescension and disregard. Flippancy."

"You see, for a long time, I was in a situation where if called upon to share I couldn't, and games afforded me a way out. Now I *can* share, as evidenced by the wine I gave you. But shit's not always running at a profit."

She continued to stare out, unresponsive. Same old thing. I watched her a second, then sat back in my chair. Slumped a little. Closed my eyes.

9.

Self-approved ambition. That's what emboldened the paper hocker and the paper pusher. But they weren't my problem. My problem was Genia's sunk capital. Not that she was drowning. Genia was no damsel in distress, with her parties and parental subsidy. Externally sustained, she didn't need me for much. The truth was, I had few reasons to believe she'd prefer me to security. My time with her was precarious, a stop on the way to wherever she saw herself going. She'd find me out eventually, and that would be that.

It was a quick favor, a game I didn't belong in. Andrew knew next to no one, so he said, and I only knew him. After he left, the game went on, and I kept beating them. Winning and winning and winning. What a recipe for disaster: in the Warehouse District, no friends, no ride home, drunk, raking in cash.

Near Canal, bystanders infested my peripherals. Descending streetcars, standing under awnings, passing on the sidewalk, they turned to me, as if with finger-guided chins:

tourists

workers

students   strippers with gym bags   bums

barkers

whores

doormen

I snaked my way past them, through them.

On the courthouse steps a man ate chicken. A pile of bones was between his feet. Never too early I guess.

-

I rested beneath a tree in the dog park on lower Burgundy. Out in the dandelioned field, a muscular girl played fetch with a young boxer. She didn't seem to notice me, maybe was hard enough not to feel threatened. One time she threw the ball into wet grass, and the dog circled and recircled the marshy area but wouldn't go in. Eventually, she went over and retrieved it for him.

The church struck top-of-the-hour chimes: six bells, and the last one lingered.

Before the park I'd stopped outside Verti Mart to call Andrew collect. After a silent moment the operator returned and said the call couldn't be put through.

I was going to tell Genia I'd been robbed. A partial truth. My bludgeoned appearance would elicit sympathy. She'd know I was broke, beaten, and walletless, but nothing about her account. I was going to have to set that straight soon. I hoped she hadn't yet tried to pay for anything.

10.

The sky'd purpled up. Down below, kids went by in blinking necklaces. Cars passed on Decatur, blaring music. Somehow my drink hadn't spilled. I turned around, saw one light on, a floor lamp in the den. Jello Dress? Nowhere to be seen.

I opened my eyes wide, blinked them a few times. Downed my drink.

Back inside, I found a note on the front door that was just an arrow pointing down to my bagged-up toiletries.

The courtyard was lit up by a floodlight that had been mounted high above the kitchen windows. A bunch of lizards and a swarm of what looked like termites had gathered around it. Descending the stairs, I saw one of the insects get close to the light, and a lizard grabbed it and disappeared into the dark.

I found another note stuck to the courtyard gate: "Good Luck Frostyface."

The restaurant's giant windows were still open. Ceiling fans spun furiously inside. The floor was noisy with the sounds of laughing diners, vintage jazz music, silverware clinking on ceramic. I didn't see anyone I knew inside. At the front, an old man slurping soup looked up at me. Then his crab-gobbling wife.

A carriage with no passengers came down Decatur. It

passed me and stopped at the water troughs by the square. This reminded me what little distance I'd covered since waking up.

I stood there and rubbed my eyes, thought about what was next. Either try the credit cards, spend the cash, or go back to begging, I figured.

-

As darkness slid over the sky like a manhole cover I walked up St. Anne, along the banquette as they say. A bit discomposed by inebriants and superficial wounds, I observed, as I went along, whittled looking kids with too-gorgeous women, beefy laughing crackers with backwards visors, drunk old folks, on the ground abandoned beads, cigarette butts, rolling cups, mule shit.

I'd decided, after looking at my ridiculous reflection in a car window, to go home and get my passport, my backup ID. Really I looked nothing like Jacob Schmidt, and any cards I'd use had probably been reported stolen by now anyway. I'd need another shower then, and I knew I would have to ask for it without having Genia's reimbursement or an explanation for my state of affairs. I'd just have to ask her for the help, make promises, brave more interrogations and acrid disapproval. Maybe I'd get a hotel. I honestly hadn't thought about it—I just needed to get the goddamned passport was the only thing on my mind.

At the intersection of Bourbon and Dumaine I passed the glitzy, techno musiced spectacle of Gay Laffite's. People out front danced and played with balloons—one whistled at me.

One block later I crossed Dauphine, and, looking up the street, saw our blue stoop sticking out into the sidewalk like a renegade tree root. A man was on the steps there, hunched over, looking out at the street.

Who might that be? Someone connected to Andrew? The guy from last time?

I needed to up the ante on my disguise. No one connected to Andrew could notice me, here, or anywhere for that matter. I might get tailed, jumped, driven further into my soily purgatory.

I turned around and went left on Dauphine, and walked to the place on St. Philip that sold chocolates and roses. On my way past Lafitte's the boys whistled at me again and called me Daddy.

He wore a white T-shirt and black jean shorts, and sat with his arms crossed, an elbow on each knee. As I moved toward him, four people were coming from the opposite direction. They had the look of middle-aged jackoffs about them: wives in Capri pants wearing regional trinkets, men with tropical shirts tucked into khaki shorts, all of them chuckling and holding big aluminum bottles of pissy American lager. When they passed the stoop, the kid leaned forward and murmured at them. In response, the men moved closer to the women and they picked up their pace, and of course cast me a suspicious look when we all went by each other. I wasn't sure what to make of that. Was the whippersnapper selling drugs?

When I got to the left gate the kid looked over at me. No surprise there. It wasn't the same guy as the day before, though. He looked back out, not needing to communicate, apparently, whatever he'd said to the foursome.

I stared down the dark walkway and wondered what Genia would say to me, what she'd say about my costume. It dawned on me that I looked like a moron, standing here dressed up and dyed white, holding chocolates and flowers. How should I explain this? I couldn't think about it—my mind was on little more than a vague estimation of how much caustic energy she'd put in my face when I asked her to fetch my passport.

Above my right shoulder, the door to one of the front units opened. Out came our neighbor, Opal, dressed in jeans and a cowboy hat, with no shirt on. That was typical, as was the young dude behind him who wore huge yellow-tinted glasses, a see-through fuchsia tank top, and a pink boa around his neck. "God," Opal said when he saw the kid on the stoop. "I should charge you people rent."

The kid looked up at him, back at the street.

Opal and Pink Boa descended the stoop and hit the sidewalk. When they were behind me, their footsteps paused. Opal's squeaky voice came squealing out. "Hello there," he said. "May I help you?"

I turned around.

His sincere expression didn't change when he saw me, a sign my disguise was working, at least in dull porch light. I saw an opportunity to get some information, and throw the stoop sitter off my trail.

"Hello there youngster," I said. "My name is Josephine and I'm from-"

"I'm sorry," he interrupted. "What was your name? Joseph Ian?"

"No, no," I said. "Josephine."

"Oh."

I tilted my head back, frowned, and widened my eyes.

"You got a problem with that, lily lips?"

"No, I just-"

"Okay, then," I said. "As I was saying, I'm here from Hattiesburg-"

"Mississippi?"

"No, dumbass! Virginia! And I'm here to see my niece Genia."

"My God. Genia, from Virginia? I thought her family all lived in Northern Louisiana and Mississippi."

"Well, you must be out of the loop, sonny."

"I must be," he said thoughtfully.

The kid began watching us.

"So, neighbor," I said, "I've been given some very unsettling information. I hear my niece has been swindled by her disreputable man-friend."

"Well," Opal said. "I don't know about that."

"Well, where is she?"

"I don't hang out with her, really, so I don't know. She's working tonight I think. I know *he's* not there."

"I see."

"I have her number. Do you need it? I feel so bad about the flowers and chocolates."

"That's all right, sonny. Just relay this message to her."

"Okay," he said.

"You tell her Mr. Hotard's on his feet, and he's coming back to set it all straight."

"Okay."

"You got that, sassypants?"

"Yes!"

The kid was memorizing my face. I knew it was time to go.

"Well, then," I said. "Thank you. I bid you good-evening."

I walked down Dumaine, with the three of them staring at me. A medley of new questions began playing in my head. How far did Andrew's bankroll reach? Was the kid connected to him after all, and looking out for me? Could Andrew afford to keep the stoop occupied? I had $130 dollars left. Where could Mr. Schmidt take me, a hotel, another restaurant, a bar? I tried to remember Genia's schedule. After a normal shift she'd be back at nine, later if she stayed out. Maybe I should go see her, go back and ring the doorbell in case she was there, wait for her on the stoop, wait somewhere else, scale the fence even though it was spiked at the top, break a window?

I meandered to Bourbon, trying to think of what to do next. I got a beer and sipped it and stared at people going by, then walked to another place and got a purple yard full of slushy bullshit and went to work on that. A few people made smartass jokes about where I was going with the flowers and chocolates. One said "The Colonel must be in the doghouse!" Each time, I smiled, and played the role of silly local eccentric who knew he'd been zinged. I started thinking about trashing what I'd been carrying, maybe getting into the candy.

Near St. Peter, my deepening inebriation, spectating and absorption of saucy heckles was interrupted by something that stood out amidst the human scenery: a pudgy young couple coming toward me, engaged in a conversation that was augmented by quarrelsome gestures. They seemed really pissed at each other—people in the streets were noticing too.

I turned away from them as they approached.

"You don't know where we are," the girl said.

"Yes I do," the guy replied, "we're on Bourbon."

"That's not what I mean. You know it's not."

"What do you mean?"

"Oh, fuck you."

"Whaaaat."

"I'm going back. By myself. Go look on your own."

"Why?"

"Leave me alone. I'll call you later."

"Jessica-"

No answer.

I looked back and saw the girl walking in the other direction, and the guy standing there watching her. He had blinking bead necklaces on, a visor, a big white shirt, plaid shorts, flip-flops. His face looked like his body—doughy, pasty, what a pizzaman starts tossing into the air.

"Howdy, señor."

He turned to me.

I smiled. "Waiting for my girl," I said, holding my roses and candy in the air.

"Huh?"

"Eh, heh, heh, heh."

He looked me over. "I wish I had some of those," he said, nodding at my wares.

"Oh yeah?"

"Do you know where I can get some?"

"Right here!" I held them out. "For $30, you can have the flowers *and* the chocolates."

"Can you just tell me where you got them?"

"Look," I said, giving upper Bourbon a lazy puppet point, "the longer you take to track *her* down, the more it's gonna cost you. And I'm not just talking about chocolates, flowers, or even thirty bucks."

He looked up the street.

"Good luck!" I said. "Stay away from her purse!"

He waved without turning. I smiled—a $5 profit, and the chocolates were probably melted.

After pocketing the money I stood there and watched more idiots going up and down Bourbon, taking pictures of each other with their rectangle phones, drinking, smoking, looking at maps. A lucky feeling began to percolate in me. Not so coincidentally, I remembered then that Mr. Schmidt had a casino membership card. And that sometimes they fronted you credit with those.

Hookers and pickpockets clogged the heart of the Quarter. Up and down the street they went, estimating marks. If you couldn't identify them by their appearances or behavior, you could by the reactions of the barkers and hot dog vendors to their passing.

The Quarter's southwest corner was peppered by the upscale—restaurants with tinted windows, uniformed greeters in front of hotels, antique shops as old as the things they sold, bars with beers from Europe and California. This area was vastly different from the northwest hotels, the northeast residencies, the southeast bauble shops.

My half-finished yard of syrup-slush in hand, I crossed Canal and ascended the steps of the old courthouse. When I opened a big glass door and entered the casino, the overbearing jingles of slot machines greeted me along with cool air and a looming tobacco stench.

Standing at the front console was a tuxedoed man whose shiny head reflected the orgy of colored lights that blinked everywhere. I gave him Mr. Schmidt's membership card and license. He returned the license with a chuckle. Another reminder of my new identity. Was I giving myself away?

"So," he said. "How's your stay in N'wahulins been?"

"So far, my friend, it's been spectacular."

He grinned and gave me a head-to-toe scan. The way he did this made me feel he saw right through my disguise. I imagined he'd press a button and there would be a descending cage, swarming security, sirens, but all he did was put a foot back and whistle. "Nice getup," he said. "I like the slacks. Pleated and *everything*."

"Thank you sir."

"You must have a tailor in town. Pants don't come out of suitcases looking like *that*."

"Well. Let's just say it's all meant to play off the beard."

He laughed, and ran the casino club card.

"Mr. Schmidt," he said, looking down at his little screen.

I cringed.

"Yes?"

"Would you like your credit line renewed?"

"Oh, absolutely. I planned on asking at the tables."

"Nah, we've got you covered here man!"

"Indeed. Thank you."

He said something into a walkie-talkie, and right away an escort emerged from the slot machine forest with my chips. There were a ton of them. This dude was a real player I guess. I put the yard down and said, "Can I leave this here?" The guy only smiled, which I guessed meant yes. The escort smiled too, and handed me my chips and led me to the poker area. I counted several hundred dollars in the racks. I should just cash these out, I thought. But it was well short of what I owed Genia, and what would that have looked like to go straight to the cashier, and where would I go when I left? Back home with only enough for a down payment on a resolution, an upgrade to a lesser circle of hell? More importantly, casino games were my bread and butter, where I flourished. A safe, controlled environment, and I had a bankroll.

At the front, I told the host I wanted a no-limit game. Immediately I was taken to a table in the back. Some kids and crusty grownups populated it, no one I recognized. None said hello to me. But they all watched me sit down.

While I was setting my chips up I threw down the cash, all except for about $40, and said, "Give me some more." The young female dealer, smiled, nodded. A couple young guys looked at each other. When the dealer had taken care of me, I scanned my competition and saw I had about a mid-level stack for the table

I had to sit out the first hand. As it played out an old Asian lady showed queens to beat some kid wearing a backwards-upside-down visor—when he saw he was beat he laughed, and showed the losing cards even though he didn't have to. The lady smiled, scooped her chips in. Another youngster said, "Had to hang in there" and Visor Boy nodded, shrugged. This relaxed me a little.

In the next hand I put up my first call holding Queen-Ten black. A couple players looked at me seriously for the first time when I jumped in. I wondered what they thought of my white hair and lopsided goatee. No one was saying anything.

I folded to a big bet after an uncooperative flop came down. As I did, a chubby-chested cocktail waitress with a tattoo on her neck came by and asked if anybody needed anything. I ordered a cognac, with a Heineken back. "Play better loose, huh?" Visor Boy said. I looked around, and saw that no one else was drinking.

Over the next several deals, I got nothing but garbage cards—I folded each time, and kept my eyes on the felt, trying not to look anxious, hoping several lay-downs out of the gate wouldn't give me a reputation for being tight. During these hands, one player busted out, and one left on his own. Both got replaced.

I was desperate to catch cards. Time was short, because Mr. Schmidt's presence had been registered at the front, which I couldn't take for granted. Furthermore, the longer I waited, the more reluctant a potential challenger would be to take me on when I finally did play, unless they really liked what they had, or were loose, or angry. Should I play a crappy hand as a smokescreen, or maybe just say screw it, make some excuse, get up, cash the chips, and walk out?

Three of a kind beat me. I'd grossly misread my opponent's play and was dumb enough to chase a spade draw. That burned me; those types of losing judgments needed to be checked, and fast.

"You tried for the flush," the victor said.

"Huh?" I looked up. It was one of the new players, some old guy with mossy white hair on his arms.

"You tried for the flush," he repeated. I detected an Eastern European accent. "A decent pair connected to the flop keeps you in. You hope I was bluffing."

He smiled, showing off a graveyard of chipped, yellow teeth. I didn't say anything, just looked back down at the felt.

The next deal went around. Two new cards came: Ace-King, both diamonds. I bumped the table $40 and everyone folded, except the guy who'd just taken me. "Oh," he said, looking around. "He folds, folds, folds, folds so much, but, now he wants to raise. He must feel lucky. Look at him. So young for such gray hair! Experienced and youthful, how impressive!"

I stayed quiet, elbows on the padding, hands clasped in front my mouth.

"Okay, mister," he said, "I play," and tossed his chips in.

The first three cards came down. Two diamonds, and I had a gutshot straight draw (needing the Jack). Not bad. If another diamond or a Jack came on the turn, I'd have him. I wasn't sure if I'd call a big bet though, since I'd learned too many times, on the last hand for instance, you went broke chasing flush draws.

I checked. So did he, without saying anything.

The Jack of Diamonds came on the turn. Beautiful. Now *he* was the one who'd made a mistake, having passed on a chance to bet me out of the hand. I felt adrenalin.

Then came some even better luck: he fixed his beady black eyes on me, and said, "I'm all-in."

"Call."

"Call?" he said. "You call?"

"Can't put these down, boss."

People murmured. "Awww shit," said Visor Boy.

After some counting, the dealer took most of my opponent's chips to match my bet.

The pile was massive. Everyone was watching to see what we'd flip:

Gel Hair   Bloated Whale

Me   Popped Collar

Quiet Grandma   10♦Q♠7♦J♦   Visor Boy
       shitload of chips

Asian Broad   Crusty Adversary
        Dealer

He turned over Queen-Two diamonds and grimaced when he saw my Ace-King of the same suit. So he *hadn't* made much of a mistake after all. He'd just been out-slugged.

"Ah, Christ," he said. "Sweet thorny-crowned savior up on *lumber*."

"Drawing dead," said the old lady next to me.

The dealer pushed the chips toward me and I began making cylinders out of them and laughing. My slain opponent, with a perplexed expression, looked back and forth between my stack and the dealer, who was shuffling the cards. "Why don't you deal the fifth card?" he said.

"You were mathematically eliminated," the dealer said. "It was pointless."

"Pointless? You still deal all five cards. For complete game. This is incomplete game. I want results voided."

"Now you're begging," I said.

"Fuck you," he stood, and pounded his fist on the table. "Do you know who I am? I am property owner. I am rich. I pay the taxes. I own this town!"

"Sir, please calm down," the dealer said.

"Look at this guy," he turned his palm up at me. "This sour-mash Santa. His mouth looks like the victim of a dog's arousal."

The dealer turned toward the front podium and raised his hand. Security came over, but when they reached the table the guy sat in his chair. It took some effort for them to uproot him; when they finally did, he shouted and flailed his limbs as they dragged him away, with more of his native vernacular, whatever it was, seeping into his speech. After they'd hauled him off someone came and took his chips. One of the kids made a joke about dividing them up, and everybody laughed. I did too. God, if only I had this kind of security at all my games.

More luck came my way after that. It was as if vanquishing the Euro had lifted a curse. I caught cards, bluffed with no consequence, took small pots, big ones, folded when someone didn't seem right. Things got fun. I was winning, cracking jokes, becoming a table mainstay. The waitress kept coming by too, with more cognacs. I started giving her chips with bigger numbers on them.

A new dealer sat down, some scrawny little man with a droopy face. He nodded hello at me, and looked down at my beard before attending to the cards. I pondered that as he shuffled. Was he onto me? People got dressed up like clowns for all kinds of reasons down here, but the look he gave made me feel visible. The red flags started fluttering again: every moment I stayed here, the odds increased I'd get found out. How long would it be before the tracking card got identified as stolen?

Two hands later I caught a straight and took a huge pot, which forced Popped Collar to buy back in. That made the scrape particularly satisfying. *Fuckin rich kid.* I didn't know exactly how much I had after that, but, in a loose estimation, it was over what I owed Genia. If that wasn't my cue to leave, then nothing was.

"Can I get a few racks?" I said to the dealer. "I'm finished tonight."

The dealer nodded, raised his hand, and said, "Two racks" to someone behind me.

"Aw, come on," Popped Collar said, "give me a chance to win it back."

"Man, I ain't getting any luckier than this tonight," I said. He laughed, nodded, looked down.

The racks came, and I filled them, stacked them, got up, tipped the dealer, and wished them all good luck.

I sat down in front of a slot machine and counted the chips. The final number put me over what I'd taken from

Genia by more than a thousand. I hesitated to go to the cashier though. Some places asked for a signature or a license for a cashout like this. It'd be better to go back home, I figured, show Genia the chips, clean up, and come back as myself with the passport.

The damp, stagnant air was as charged with heat as at midday. Cars were out, and people, at a rate that told me the night was still young. Walking down the steps I felt tired, heavy-headed. I sat on a cement bench at the bottom and thought my situation over. Genia had to be home by now. But I was pretty goddamned drunk, and too fatigued to endure her wrath. And what about the stoop sitter?

In any event, I'd gone as far as I could with Mr. Schmidt. I knew that. Now it was a liability having him on my person. I took out the wallet and tossed it into a trashcan by the bench, something that caught the attention of a few passersby.

11.

Our building could be described as traditional French Quarter: stone homes with narrow walkways designed to thwart invasions. Identical gates about ten feet high blocked off the walkways and were topped by rusty spikes. I approached our side, and rang the doorbell.

The gate didn't buzz. For a moment I thought she might not be there, but then the door opened and she peeked out. I waved at her.

Instead of waving back, or ducking back in and buzzing the gate, she descended our side stoop and started down the walkway.

She wore a T-shirt and sweatpants. No shoes. Her hair was all messy. She looked concerned. Maybe preoccupied was the word.

She stopped a few paces from the gate, and after giving me a somewhat unsympathetic up-and-down, raised her eyebrows, put her hands on her hips, and said, "Tough night at the office?"

"Hey, what's up?" I said. "Why didn't you buzz me in?"

"Is it true?"

Not sure what she meant, I went right into my story.

"Genia," I said, "I had an incident. I was robbed."

"Is it true?"

"Is what true?"

"He said you started making stupid bets and insulting people. That you were drunk and out of control."

"Who's 'he?'"

She cocked her head.

"Who, Genia?"

"He said one guy wanted to kill you, and he almost did."

"Genia-"

"I believe it. Look at you!"

"Genia, go back in and buzz the gate."

"All my money's gone!" she said in a sharp, piercing voice. This change in tone surprised me, as much as the revelation of what she knew. My feeling of surprise, though, quickly turned to irritation.

"All of your *what* is *what*?" I said. "How should I know what's what?"

"Huh?"

"Huh what?"

"Adam, what the hell are you saying?"

"What are *you* saying?"

She exhaled through her nose, pressed her lips together, and shook her head.

A horse carriage clopped by. One block away, music came from Laffite's. Further down I heard boat horns, a pennywhistle.

"So that's how you make a living?" she said. "Gambling?"

"What? Gambling?"

"Down on your luck? Needing a big score?"

"No, Genia."

"I'd have paid for more things," she said. "If this was the alternative, you little weasel shit!"

"Hey, I was at work, I swear!"

"Really," she said. "So how'd you get like this?"

"A pre-foreclosure sale gone wrong. Unruly clientele."

"What?"

"Prep work for the morning crew, Genia. High-stress doubles. Markets in different time zones. Lots of pressure on us. Hard sells. You know my job!"

"Oh my God."

"What did he tell you?" I said. "Is he back there in his place?"

"No, Adam, he's not."

"Well, where is he, then?"

"I don't know."

"Well, his friends will know who's got the money."

"No they won't," she said.

"No?" I said. "You two seem pretty close all of a sudden. How are you so sure?"

She crossed her arms and looked past me.

"Listen to what you're saying. You're admitting your lie."

I exhaled.

"Okay," I said, "I didn't go in last night. Alright? Andrew asked me if I'd go to a game, so I went."

"Adam-"

"Andrew lost early, and *I* won the game. Next thing I know, I'm walking to a car with his friends and I get tackled-"

"Adam, you used my money."

"Listen. If he told you all those things and left before I was robbed then dumped uptown, he was involved."

"The fact that you found a way to take it out-"

"Genia, did you hear me? Robbed, and dumped uptown."

She didn't reply.

"Andrew knows who has your money," I said.

She looked at me.

"And a shitload of mine."

"Jesus, you are a fucking idiot."

"It was just a game, Genia. A high-stakes game. I needed a big bankroll. I wanted to surprise you. I should have surprised you. My plan worked. I sextupled your money!"

"Adam, I've got to think," she said. "You can't stay here tonight."

"What?"

"Don't try to scale the fence, either. You'll hurt yourself. And even if you get over, I won't open the doors anyway."

"Dammit Genia," I said. "I pay for half the expenses, you have to let me in. It's half my place."

She glared at me and leaned forward where she stood,

arms still crossed.

"I don't fucking give a shit!"

While I tried to think of a response she reached into her sweatpants pocket and took out a wad of miscellaneous things: torn pieces of paper, a post-it note, cash, a business card. "Here," she said, coming closer, and handing me a twenty through the bars. "Take this."

"Genia," I said, "can I come in and get cleaned up? Change my clothes?"

"Go to the hostel," she put her hair behind her ear and looked down. "You can't stay here."

"Where is it?"

"Find out."

"When should I be back?"

She turned and went back down the walkway.

"*Genia.*"

She went inside. I heard the door lock.

"Ask *him* for your money, goddammit!"

The hostel. That's where she was sending me. And I'd forgotten to tell her about my lost wallet. Could I even get into the hostel without identification?

I looked at the top of the gate. She was right about climbing over. Even at my sprightliest, it was a perilous endeavor.

What the hell should I do now? Should I ring Andrew's button?

Andrew.

The first time I met him was right after we'd moved in, at a party in our place overpopulated by neighbors and Genia's friends. I remember him standing in our living room with a glass of beer, and me telling him about my bad cards, and my bad luck, and how bad luck moves around New Orleans like an oscillating fan in a roomful of candles. "Don't mention any of that to Genia," I said. "We're kind of new together, on the up and up." He asked if by new together I meant living or being together, and I said both.

At that he smiled, and said, "You know, I play a little bit too. But I play like hell."

"Yeah?"

"Give me your number. I'll keep you in mind for the next game."

"Here," I said. "Let me give you the landline."

The twenty fell out of my hands and sidewound to the ground. I picked it up, and began ringing Andrew's bell. After about a minute pressing the button over and over, I felt a hand on my shoulder. I turned, expecting it to be him, but instead saw a youngster in a white tank top holding a phone to his ear. He asked me my name; when I gave it he asked if I had a cigarette, and when I said no he took out a pack of cigarettes and asked if I had a lighter. I said no again, and he took a cigarette from the pack, fished a lighter from his pocket, lit the cigarette, took a puff, and asked me if I had any change.

"No, man, I don't."

"Well then what *do* ya have?"

"Not much."

"Not much? So what are ya doin here?"

"I'm waiting for someone."

"Me, too," he said. "My girl's picking me up on the corner over there."

He pointed toward Burgundy.

Not knowing what to make of him, I walked over to the stoop and sat down. He came over too and stood in front of me and took another drag of his cigarette.

"I need to sit on *this* side of you," he said, pointing to my right. "Scoot over. You're kinda *broad*."

I moved.

He sat down, and slapped his phone shut without saying goodbye to anybody.

A horse carriage pulled up to the Burgundy stop sign. Nine people were inside—the driver and eight tourists. The decrepit mule pulling the carriage was laboring hard, bobbing its head desperately with every lurch of the hoof.

"Fifty bucks per couple," I said, nodding at the carriage. "For a quick status high."

"So, what did you used to have?" he said.

"Huh?"

"I said, what'd ya used to *have*?"

He flicked his cigarette, but no ashes came off. A little amused by that, I leaned back. "Well," I said. "I *used* to be in real estate. Recently too."

"Oh yeah?" He looked me over. "Must be a rough market."

"The roughest."

He turned toward Dauphine.

I couldn't make out much on his person, only what seemed like the cigarette pack in his left pocket.

By the time he turned back, my eyes were on the street.

"So," I said. "Ya got a smoke for me?"

"Nah."

I laughed.

Now the kid was annoying me. Where was this going? He wasn't intimidating me, making solicitations, pleading for assistance. I didn't believe he was waiting for his girlfriend. I decided to go back to Andrew's doorbell. When I stood up, he adjusted his belt and stared at me. I noticed something under his shirt, right above the belt buckle.

He tapped it. Smiled. Then he lifted his shirt and showed me.

This wasn't a hold-up. I knew that. But I couldn't figure out what he wanted. Was he affiliated with Andrew, did he know me from some poker game? Did Genia put him up to it? Did he just want the stoop?

"Alright, man," I said. "I'll leave. But I ain't done comin' around. Spread the word."

He took on a look of concentration. Nodded his head. Condescending asshole.

12.

A blaring horn faded up Canal, gone by the time I'd opened my eyes.

I was still on the bench—passed out for how long? God, what an invitation to get robbed or arrested. I counted the chips. All there still.

An elderly couple walking by made lemon-sour faces at me. Some endgame.

-

Across Canal, sloppy merrymakers flourished in the propped-up district. The anonymity of this crowd relaxed me. Mental cobwebs began clearing. Questions arose: What time was it? Should I go back home, just plop down in the first anonymous place? Could I go back into the casino and cash enough chips for a hotel?

On Royal, onlookers surrounded a hive of police cars, the largest of which was a big boxy paddy wagon parked just off Bienville. All the siren lights made it look like some kind of club scene. The police were unloading detainees from the wagon and lining them up on the sidewalk outside the station. All of them were men and they all looked downcast and hostile. Except one: near the back of the line, the guy who'd been dragged out of the casino. My benefactor. He had the same defiant demeanor as before, talking animatedly to the people around him, flailing his arms like he was swatting at mosquitoes. Everyone ignored him but it didn't seem to tamp down his ebullience, though when a cop came by he settled down, only to pick back up when the cop moved on.

A thought came to me as I watched him: what if I asked him to cash in my chips for a fee? I could go into the casino with him and stand off to the side while he went to the cashier. Something told me he'd do it, that he'd see it as restitution for an unfair loss. Maybe it was a stupid, drunken idea. Maybe it'd be better to ask some random person. Or steal the wallet of someone I looked like.

The line started moving. I got a sense of urgency to act.

-

"*You,*" he said, "I should have known you by your smell by now. What are you doing here?"

"I've come to rescue you," I said.

"Rescue me? Oh my sweet prince."

"Judging from the time you were taken out of the casino," I said, "until the time your paddy wagon arrived, I assume you were in there for a while-"

"What are you saying?" he said. "Paddy what? Paddy Power?"

I paused.

"Didn't you say you were a valuable property owner?"

"Yes," he said. "I could buy and sell you, Motherfucker Ace High Flush! Paddy Cakes!"

"Well, listen. I need you to cash in my casino chips, if you're interested. You can make some money from it."

"Me, cash your chips?"

"That's right."

He raised his eyebrows and stuck his bottom lip out at the men around him.

"Why is this?"

"That's my business. I can't do it, let's just leave it at that."

"Okay," he said. "I will. But only if you bail me out."

"What?"

"And I'll take ten percent of your proceeds."

"Uhh."

"Let's make that fifteen."

"Well-"

The line kept moving. I had to stay back. Before he went on ahead, he turned and smiled. "Think about it," he said. "We'd be good friends!"

-

A herd of Chiefs fans wandered up the street, festooned in their team's regalia. Their boys were in town to play the Saints and an increase in their numbers meant it was the end of the week—I guess a general swell in the tourist population did, too. One of them, some red-faced grandpa, came up to me and put his team's necklace on me. "Go Chiefs!" he said, laughing, and slapped my face a little then rejoined his friends off to the side, who were laughing too. I watched them wobble off, and thought, too bad he doesn't look like me. This observation made me consider how desperate I was, what I might be capable of, how close to arrest recklessness was bringing me, how hard it was to gain traction, how I didn't have a place to stay, was losing my ability to get new games together, and the idea of just leaving Genia for good and never paying her back? No, I couldn't do that. Couldn't. I'd never get away from doing something like that—it'd chase me forever.

-

At the front desk I told them I wanted to talk to the obnoxious European. They said I'd have to be a little more specific.

-

When my new friend saw me he got up off a bench on the back wall and came to the bars. The cop who escorted me returned to the front, strangely enough.

I searched the cell for anyone who might know me.

"So," he said, showing off those gruesome teeth, "couldn't resist, eh?"

"Did you think about my deal?" I said.

"Did you think about mine?"

"Yes," I said.

"Good," he said. "Wise of you."

I put my hands in my pockets, and leaned in close to him. "Um," I said, "do you think I could sleep at your place tonight?"

"God, why?" his voice rose. "We are strangers!"

"I have no place to stay."

"Sweet Lucifer."

"The other thing is, I have no cash. At all. Only chips."

His eyes narrowed.

"Ah, you are a thief and a liar, aren't you? A dirty thief who belongs in here!"

"*Ssshhh*" I looked up to the front.

"Those chips belong to me," he said. "I am their rightful owner. But I am generous. Weak-mindedly so. Because of this, I will create a chance for you to beat me fair and square. You have to play in a private game with me."

"A private game?"

He leaned through the bars and squawked down the hall. "Officers!"

I pushed him backwards. "God, you idiot, what the hell is wrong with you? I don't have any ID."

"Give them some of the chips," he said. "It's the only way

to get me out. How do you not know this?"

"What? How many?"

"Not so much you can't play a game with me."

An officer came up to us, holding a sandwich, and looking offended we'd rousted him in the middle of his feeding. It took him two syllables to say "What?"

"Sir," I said, with no time to second guess myself, "whatever my friend did, can I just pay for it right here? He is my poker coach and I know he is ill-tempered. He's had too much to drink and that's my fault."

"Well," the officer said, "we're fining him for disturbing the peace, but we haven't set any kind of fee."

"Sir," I said. "I am a longtime resident of the French Quarter, and on more than one occasion I have benefited from the protection of your law enforcement. I have been meaning to do this for a while, but now is as good a time as ever to give something back, to break with the old refrain of empty rhetoric, if you will."

I reached into my pocket, grabbed all the chips I could, and presented them. "This remuneration," I said, "should be used in accordance with the budget of the New Orleans Police Department."

He looked down.

"Officer," I said, "let me speak frankly. Things have been too shitty in this town for too long for us to compromise ourselves over the well-being of others who are not in a position to help us the way we are able to help each other.

Apologies to Jesus, let him come down here to the Vieux Carre, and show us how we're supposed to survive. How about we go up there, and say, 'Hey, Goddammit, this is how we do it.' We! Understand?"

He lowered his sandwich a little.

I shook the chips with my right hand, pressed my left hand to my chest, and nodded.

"*We.*"

"Are you always so good with money?"

"Kiss my ass."

Neither of us mentioned going to the casino. We didn't talk at all, actually; once we were outside, he just said "Let's catch a ride." I nodded, and we went to the streetcar stop on Poydras. When a car came, he paid my fare.

While he stared at some girls a few rows up I turned around, and watched the skyline of the city contract.

The car scraped up the tracks, stopping at times for lights or to let off passengers. Before long, we were the only ones on board.

Beneath one of the seats close to the front, I saw a pack of Marlboro Lights. "Think there's any smokes in there?" I said, pointing at it.

He didn't look. "I've already thought about this," he said. "No need to bother."

"Why not at least check?"

He turned to me.

"When was the last time you saw a pack of stray smokes not empty?"

"Um-"

"Unless it was on top of a coffee table, or countertop?"

I was quiet.

His bobbing head echoed the bumps in the road. I thought about this guy, contemplated his stoicism, his rep-tile-dry skin, why he'd agreed to bargain with me. All of this quickly made me uncomfortable.

"You don't know my name," I said.

He looked at me, and down at my necklace.

"I call you Chief. Okay with you?"

"Sure," I said, examining the necklace for the first time. "But what's your name?"

"Ivan."

"Okay. Ivan."

We moved uptown, into the Garden District. Soon we began to see houses with huge pillars, manicured foliage, driveways lit up by green, yellow and purple lights.

Just as the big, chaperoning oak trees started to appear, Ivan pulled the cord and rang the bell.

When the doors opened, the driver turned his head and gave us a little nod.

The car rolled up St. Charles and disappeared, leaving us on the embankment in the middle of two empty streets. We crossed in the direction of the river, and Ivan led me to a brick-faced apartment building that looked nice from the sidewalk, but after walking up a rickety flight of stairs I saw it was kind of a dump, with barred front windows and doors that were chipped and painted different colors. All the lights in the building, even the porch lights, were off. Only one unit had anything out front of it, a place at the end of the upper walkway with a lawn chair and doormat decorating the porch area.

Ivan opened a door next to the decorated unit, walked into it, and turned a light on. While he fussed around inside, I looked down at a parking lot that was empty except for a black truck. Several houses surrounded the lot, some with light in their windows.

He came back out and motioned me in.

It was a storage locker, full of heat, a sharp metallic smell, shelves stocked with cleaning supplies, a fan, coiled-up cords and buckets on the ground, a light bulb hanging from the ceiling. In the center was a small cot, which I presumed Ivan had just set up.

He turned the fan on. "I'll wake you in the morning," he said, looking around the room. "You can help me at Lafayette, then we'll play the game."

"Lafayette? The city?"

He shut the door without answering.

I stood there in the dark, not wanting to think about anything. The room had one tiny window. Iron bars quartered it into four equal sections which made glowing squares on the opposite wall.

I heard clicking beneath me. Scraping, tapping. Familiar sounds. Knowing exactly what it was, I turned the light on anyway, and sure enough saw roaches all over the ground—the big ones too, that were about the size of wine bottle's cork. They didn't go scurrying away either, like they knew I was nothing to be afraid of.

Glancing around, I still couldn't see any place with light on inside, or anything at all that would indicate an occupied unit. Everything was dark, empty.

Finally the door opened, just a crack.

He rubbed one eye with his fist.

"What is it, Chief?"

"Can I sleep in here?" I said.

"Why?"

"There's lots of roaches in the shed."

"I have them too! Go, I wake you tomorrow."

He started to shut the door.

"Wait," I said.

"What?"

"Do you have anything to drink?" I said.

"Something to drink?"

I pulled out a chip out of my pocket.

"I'll pay for it."

Ivan stared down at the chip. "Sure," he said. "Wait here."

He opened the door a little, and turned a light on. I watched him walk across a junky living room over to a kitchen area so small it seemed more like a tiny worksta-tion built into the wall.

"Want this alligator pear?" he said.

"This what?"

He pointed to a pineapple on the counter.

"Fresh from store."

"Well, alright. Thanks."

He nodded, then went into a cupboard, and took out a half-empty bottle of brown stuff.

"Like Old Granddad?" he said.

"Not sure," I said

He came over and handed everything to me, and I gave

him the chip. He looked at the chip, and up at me, as if remembering our deal. In a move that reminded me of Kevin in the restaurant, a tiny bit of hostility flared, and was quickly smothered by something more congenial.

"Hungry?" he said, smiling. "Want a little shrimp?"

"Shrimp?"

He went to his fridge and took out a plastic container. When he handed it to me, I saw it read "Fresh Chicken Livers" on the side. Inside was a heap of orangish-gray shrimp that smelled awful. But I took them.

"Thanks, Ivan."

"How much more is in there?" he said, nodding at my pockets.

"I'll tell you tomorrow," I said, taking a step back.

"Ah, you sneaky person. I am being too generous with you."

At that, he shut the door. But the living room light stayed on.

I sat atop the staircase that descended into the parking lot and went to work on the shrimp, which I knew I'd never have touched if I were sober. It was messy work since they weren't fully cooked, and since Ivan didn't offer me any napkins. He didn't offer a knife for the pineapple either, for that matter, or a glass for the whiskey. I didn't really give a shit.

When I'd finished the shrimp I wiped my hands on my pants, left everything except the whiskey outside Ivan's door, and went to my new room. Before I entered, I noticed holes in the bottoms of mine and Ivan's doors and an extension cord connecting one place to the other.

I stared out of the window awhile, down at the parking lot, and the houses and trees that lorded over it. The fan went back and forth, back and forth, whirring, cooling me down, mussing my hair, leaving me alone, coming back again. It was noisy, though it didn't drown out the sound of the roaches.

-

I felt a little unsettled imagining a nightmarish vision of Ivan's face appearing in the window, with a burst of scary-movie music. Some of the roaches were crawling across it, and making shadows in the glowing squares on the wall. Some of them were even flying. The buzzing of their wings was a grotesque, high-pitched noise. I thought about getting up and killing all that I could. But I was just too tired. So tired. I knew they'd start crawling on me before long. At least they didn't bite.

13.

In the next to darkest moments, before you're out, survivalism seems like a matter of more than instinct—it's about imposing your will, inwardly and outwardly, and success is measured through its economies of scale.

Bad jobs, drugs. A bad road. I got off it, took another gamble, developed a skill, got good at it, wanted to prove I could keep on, went from coast to coast on the new path. Still was on that path. Drowning on that path?

I saw the Coast Guard story, the one about finding the circling floaters, as two possible metaphors: going back and forth until you found death, or going around in circles because the currents made you. Could I found anything upon either? Which was true? Did it matter?

I needed a viable analogy. Structure. Until now I'd been kowtowing to luck good or bad and never knowing it. Not until I saw all of it.

Maybe it's this: you set root, grow, and bear fruit, which ripens, falls, and rots, and the seeds get blown about until they find new soil. And the process repeats. For the lucky ones.

14.

Today there weren't any *new* funerals, but a couple of times he moved aged bones from the internment wall into family tombs, and we had importations of bodies that'd been buried in other cemeteries (he said this was common). He didn't want me helping with the bodies. He had his system down, he told me, and all I'd do was interfere. I wasn't complaining. Who wanted to work with spoiled flesh? I was fine with the job he gave me: pick up trash.

Most of the day I was in the southwest corner, smoking cigarettes at the base of a magnolia tree. Peach and moss-colored tombs surrounded me there, all of them with high walls that reached up to the magnolia's full branches. That made for plenty of shade. I came here several times, and each time I did, it was never long before Ivan accosted me. He was always angry when he found me here. Why the listlessness, he'd ask, why the lounging?

Well, for starters, there was -

Genia

cash   games

Ivan   Andrew

trashed identification

disappearing chips

gray shrimp for dinner
flying roaches
a rotting pineapple

a burning cigarette

Most of the bodies were buried above ground, if that is even how you would say it, because down here the earth gets the spits and vomits corpses in clammy weather. That didn't mean there weren't a few caskets stuck into the wet soil, which made me wonder how you said *caveat emptor* in Creole. As for the above-ground tombs, limited space in the yard, coupled with a New Orleanian tendency to allot one tomb for an entire family, meant a lot of cramming went on. Some of them housed generations of bodies, with room for more made possible by internment, an iron-wrought word that means the beef-jerkifying and shoe-boxing of carcasses.

I was waiting. Why? There were things I could have done after all—for instance, I could have insisted Ivan go to the casino with me first, or gone myself for a small cashout, or abandoned the idea altogether, or called the casino and asked how many chips I could cash without an ID, or begged Genia for my passport, but somehow I felt that I'd made a deal and was bound to it. As for whatever affair he was concocting, I knew I'd buy in for as little as possible, throw the game, let his friends win, and then be off to

109

Harrah's with him. Then we'd be done.

That said, according to Ivan, I could have hookups for future games through him. I had to consider this. Even if casino poker was preferable for security, I had to consider my past sometimes, being spotted, having to move on fast or go underground. The games could be a valuable supplement or backup, all risks considered. Another thing to factor in was, now that I'd been gone from Genia awhile I had to consider the ramifications of a prolonged absence. Would Genia call the police? Change the locks? More than anything else, she was probably worried about how it looked that I'd stolen her money, lost it, and disappeared. Her rich parents might sick detectives on me, or private security. If that happened I'd really be found out—even a new city might not help then. I smoldered inside to think about that, and to think of Andrew enjoying himself, fancying himself the storm that leveled me, free to plot ambitious plays now that I'd been taken care of. Maybe I needed Ivan. So I had to wait.

Up in the tree, wind-blown leaves blinked sunlight. I exhaled smoke and watched it dissipate upward, outward, into the leaves, gone.

A small red cardinal came hopping along one of the tree's low-jutting branches. It shot quick glances at the ground, the tombs, me, then fluttered down to my feet and came so close I could see its blotchy black face and hear its tiny claws crunching the leaves. A gust of wind burst through the area, wheezing through the magnolia and kicking up old leaves; the bird fluttered a little, landed, continued to scour the ground. Eventually it picked up a stick about the size of my cigarette and vanished.

A pair of old men came scuttling along a walkway close by. One had a bucket, the other a hose he dragged noisily on the concrete. They set their things up in front of a huge marble tomb not too far from me. Next to the tomb was a water hookup. One guy attached the hose, filled up his bucket, took it over to the tomb and began scrubbing the walls with a sponge. The other took a can of paint and a brush from a shopping bag and began touching up an iron gate.

I looked back up into the tree.

Someone looking at my situation might ask, why play at all? What kind of income was it, why constantly put yourself at risk? Into tight spots? All good questions. Circled in and circumscribed is the answer, going back and forth and sinking and being blown about all at once within vague boundaries.

"Why do you cower here?"

I opened my eyes.

There he was, angry again, as if I were on the payroll.

"Why do I what?"

"You think you're clever trying to hide," he said, "but I can see your poofy smoke puffs."

"I'm not hiding, dude."

He paused a moment, studied me.

"Do you know," he said, "that when a person talks, they are either displaying or interacting?"

"You've told me this."

"Only you would rather cower than display."

"Yes."

"And when you do work up balls to interact, because you are a youngster and because your generation is chickenshit, you fail in your attempts."

"Yes, Ivan."

"Do you know how pathetic this is?"

"No, Ivan. Why don't you tell me? Again?"

"Some people see limitations," he said, looking around. "In themselves, in others. Some see few. By choice, maybe not."

"You know," I said, "I really don't know what *any* of that means."

He looked back at me.

"Come on," he said, motioning me over. "I need help."

—

Drops of sweat trickled down his face, and he was half-consciously looking at the shells of some sunflower seeds I'd spit on the ground. When he saw the shells earlier he cursed at me and told me to clean them up, which I never did.

Many of the tombs had an ethereal air about them that was consecrated by old architecture. Like churches. Sometimes clovers sprouted from cracked mortar. They were decorated by broken nameplates, chiseled-in poetry, flower-holders (almost always flowerless), Virgin Marys, angel babies with wings. "Look at these little houses," I said. "The rust, the chipping, everything so worn away. Is the air corrosive or something?"

"No," he said, "time is."

We kept on walking.

He was frustrating me now. All this silence. And the heat. Where was this going? And what was up with our game? I decided to play some offense, get him going. "Ivan," I said, "why do you work here?"

"Why do I work here?"

"Yeah. This can't be what you envisioned for yourself. For your life."

He stopped, and eyed me with a solemn expression.

"That's my business."

"Well, yeah," I said. "I know."

We stood there for a moment. I listened to wind streaming through the trees, felt the sun that was straight overhead.

"Ivan, why are we out here?" I said, rubbing my neck. "This is killing me."

"Why would she do this?" he blurted out. "Surrender her life for a chance on you? It makes no sense."

That again.

"Have you ever met a single 19-year old girl?" I said. "Right out of the house, whose parents can foot the bill for a place away from her dorms, in the Vieux Carre, who's got a guy she's into?"

"But still, the sense to think it through."

"Sense? Christ. We live in a world where women drown their babies, marry 90-year old billionaires, cheat on their husbands with schoolchildren, and steal their roommates' clothes and hide them between their mattresses. Now tell me what the hell sense even *is* to them."

"Well," he said, looking at the ground. "I guess she thinks there's always money to fall back on."

I started to reply, but reconsidered. Clearly I'd revealed too much of myself already.

A hearse pulled up to the front gates. When Ivan saw it he moved by me, bumping my shoulder as he passed, probably on purpose. I watched him talk to the driver for a moment then went into the shed, the graveyard's de facto office. If he needed help, let him come fetch me again.

Inside the shed was

a desk   file cabinets   a television

                                                                    chairs

a giant round table   a cabinet full of liquor

I took a bottle of gin from the liquor cabinet and turned the television on.

—

He came in, dripping with sweat. His hands were dirty. "You ready?" he said, looking at the bottle then at me. I braced for more of his scolding but he turned and left without saying anything else.

We locked all but one gate, strolled the grounds, pulled trash bags from bins, made sure no lingering visitors lurked about, threw the bags into a dumpster, shut the shed up, locked the last gate, started down Prytania toward the big street.

I looked up at the trees that swayed like they were underwater.

"Hey, Chief," he said.

"What?"

"I got another dream for you. I just remembered it."

"Yeah?"

"I dreamed I could see timers above everyone's head."

"See what?"

"Clocks counting time down," he said. "To show how long a person had left to live. I saw people with big numbers, some with little ones. Everyone on an airplane with one number. Sad things. Very young people with many preceding zeroes."

"Yeah?"

"I saw a young couple with the exact same number. Should that make you happy or sad?"

"I'm not sure"

He stopped.

"Listen, stupid pie. Do you not see what this dream means?"

"What?"

"That people are blind to what hangs above their heads. Their dark-cloud numerical destinies."

I didn't answer.

He walked on ahead, turned right on 6th and picked up his pace (I figured he needed to use the bathroom), but then he stopped close to St. Charles and started looking at something in the gutter.

When I reached him, I saw what it was.

"Dove pigeon," he said.

The thing was just a shell, with eyes sunk into its skull, frayed feathers, claws that clutched nothing.

"Been dead awhile. All dried out."

I kicked it into a storm drain.

"You're nice to the gators," he said, and scurried on ahead again.

Back at his place, I walked through the open door, sat on

the ratty, ducktaped couch, and grabbed his bottle of Highland Mist from the coffee table. I took a nice gulp and went over to the window. As usual, nothing was in the parking lot except for Ivan's black truck.

In the bathroom, the toilet flushed. The fan went off. Before he came back out, though, I heard an odd noise in the bedroom, a kind of thudding-jingle sound, like when you drop a coin on top of other coins. What was that?

"I'm lighter," he said, rubbing his belly as he came down the hallway.

"Disgusting."

He sat down, and the couch cushions wheezed. "Did you know" he said, looking at the ceiling, "that when New Orleans floods, water forces manhole covers out of their holders?"

"Yes."

"So that if you walk around in the floodwater you might fall down? *Ffttt.* Like a trap door, into the pipe system underground."

"You told me that already."

"Okay, then," he said, sitting up and looking at me. "How about poker? Almost time for our game!"

"When?"

He poured scotch into a coffee mug, sipped it, and looked back at me with a half-smirk on his face, lips glistening. As if powered by its own slimy momentum, the smirk became a big smile that showed off those nasty teeth.

"You've been laying lots of eggs," he said. "You know that, cuckoo bird?"

"Huh?"

"There is a story in you," he said. "You are like pot pie. The scalding truth beneath your flaky, concealing crust. Isn't that right? Isn't that why you started out with gray hair which now is almost all brown a day later?"

"Yes, Ivan. So are we eating pot pie? And what about the game?"

"Why don't you clean yourself up and we'll talk about food?"

"Fine."

I got up and walked down the tight, cluttered hall that led to his bedroom. Wooden beams crackling beneath my feet made me think about the decrepitude of the building, and the empty units all around us. We were alone here. Summer break for students, Ivan had said. I had a hard time believing that. First of all it was September, and also I knew from experience college kids aggressively sublet their places in the summer. One of those places was where I first landed, way up by Tulane—it's what led to meeting Genia at Superior Grill.

In the bedroom, I saw that between the bathroom door and the bedroom closet, a small door I'd found locked earlier was open a crack—I took a peek inside, and saw shirts, pants, coats, nothing out of the ordinary, until I looked down, and saw a heap of jewelry.

A rose-colored pendant was on top. I picked it up, and held it to the light of the lone window. On its underside an inscription read *To Mary—Always and Forever. Gabriel. 1993.*

Was he robbing the stiffs? If so, why keep the loot here like this? And why leave the door open? Did he want me to see it? Was he testing me?

When I turned the shower on the small room quickly filled with steam. This low visibility, combined with sounds of splashing water and running pipes, made me feel anonymous, and comfortable. I started scrubbing my beard, my hair, cleaning my scrapes and cuts, and thinking more about what I'd just seen. A chain of logic emerged, played out, underwent some revision. Then, this came: **For all his condescension, Ivan underestimates my permissive disposition, not detecting a deep-seeded ability to slash and burn my way through all kinds of brush. He's wrong about his silly dream. The real lesson it offers is that anyone can be in control of anyone else's clock if they want to be. Another thing: earlier today, some stupid oaf, awkward as hell, tripped over a root and fell into some mud. I smiled when it happened, and turned away when he got up. Lessons were there, too: become founderous to the unobservant, stay unobserved.**

Never mind being afraid of him though. He'll never find you. And later you can think about how to prepare for if he does. So whatever happens in the poker game,

when you get back here and it's just you two, hit him over the head with a brick, a rock, a shovel, tie him up, gag him, and take that shit in the closet. It'd be better, easier, than just camping out and waiting for him to leave so you could break in.

You didn't believe him when he told you about the missing tenants. Now you see that exploiting the circumstance means more than the truth.

When I'd toweled off, I went to the mirror and saw my face, a dark blur in the wet surface. A bellowing noise came from out front. I snapped my head sideways. Ivan was singing along with the television.

I looked back to the mirror.

Drops of water started sliding down, streaking the film away, clearing the surface little by little, revealing more and more of my face. I watched until impatience had me expedite things.

15.

Death as a sea voyage is part of Celtic mythology, but on the I-10 sea dreams are less about eternal journeys than they are riding currents, drifting, bobbing, cresting, peaking, crashing, advancing on the ground, upon structures, in little bursts, great big gushes. In New Orleans, the sea competes with lakes, rivers, tributaries. A lot comes in. A lot doesn't get out. Sometimes it festers, rots, erodes, reconstructs. Sometimes there's a bright side—a river break, after all, saturated uptown with the soil it needed to become the Garden District.

My Irish line sailed to New York and drifted to Northern California before ending up in Los Angeles. They were gamblers, drinkers, smokers. Uneducated. Half my father's side. Religion meant to earn, to survive, to build, but this line never built so much as they stressed the difficulties of building. They were funny, though. Forgiving too. One time, during an early November evening I took a jack-o-lantern off our porch, walked out to the street, and rolled it down our hill. After a few seconds of fun watching it bounce along, I saw, at the foot of the hill, my father's car appear, and make a dramatic swerve. That was some bad luck. Thing is, when your father doesn't work for someone, you never really know his hours.

I ran into my room and sat on my bed. He came in

and found me there, sweating, out of breath, staring at the wall. "You know anything about a pumpkin bouncing down the hill," he said, smiling, "looked a lot like one that was on the porch this morning?"

16.

*T**ap TAP tap*
A double-hook contraption by the bathroom door had a top hook that was long and elegant, old-timey, with little swirls etched into the metal and a curvaceous upturn at the end.

Knock knock

Beneath that was a utility hook, an artless half-circle. Something for a working stiff hoping shower steam would smooth out his wrinkly clothes, or to hang onto for balance while urinating.

"Let's go, Chief."

I looked at the liquid in my mug, sloshed it around a little, smelled it.

"Chief-"

"Hold on."

Knock knock.

"Chief."

"Alright! Jesus."

I unlocked the door.

He came barging in, excitable and red-faced, stuffed into a small jean jacket that hardly suited the weather. "You drunk?" he said, peering into my mug.

"No."

"Have some more, then."

I tried to get around him, but he grabbed me and started hopping up and down like some raffish little troll.

"Chief drinking firewater! Ha ha ha!"

"You know what, Ivan?" I said, shaking free of him. "You're a linguistic genius."

"Yeah?"

"Yeah. You're a *linguinius*."

Out front he had a box of candles on the coffee table. When I'd asked what they were for, he said electric light would draw attention.

-

We saw them through the 6th Street gate, inside the yard already, milling about by the shed. Three of them. One motioned us over to the corner of 6th and Prytania. When we got there, a ladder appeared from behind the wall, right where a massive elm tree's branches reached far out over the sidewalk. The thing made a loud, clangy sound hitting the ground. Ivan rushed over to it, set it up, scaled it, straddled the wall, swung the ladder over, and disappeared, somehow managing the candles the whole time. After a moment it came back over for me.

I thought about running. Going back to Ivan's, getting the jewelry, vanishing.

A car passed, oblivious to me.

I looked at the ladder.

They stood in a patch of ugly mudgrass between the shed and a series of decrepit tombs. One was a diminutive man in a dress shirt tucked into belted khaki shorts, one a skinny man in jeans and a windbreaker, one an uncommonly tan mammoth in overalls. The one with the windbreaker carried a suitcase. He had a bony face, and dotty little eyes. He glanced away when we made eye contact; so did the one wearing the dress shirt, who had fragile, almost sickly posture. He looked cowed, deferential, like someone who for safety always kept an olive branch in his back pocket.

The oaf was smoking a cigarette. He took a drag and exhaled slowly, and it made his brown head look like a fuming cigar butt.

"This is the Chief," Ivan said. "Chief, meet the Georges."

No one nodded, or stuck their hand out.

"The Georges?" I said.

"We're all named Gee-orge," the big guy said, and smiled, with more smoke oozing out of his mouth.

We seated ourselves in silence. Ivan set up the candles, lit a few, and went about taping several layers of newspapers over the windows. Three packs of cards were on the table, two wrapped in plastic, next to chips that had come from

Skinny George's suitcase. I traded my chips for some of the house's. The others bought in with cash. No one made any comment about the way I bought in.

The table was tight. Not a lot of elbow room. I had Olive Branch George to my right, Skinny George across from me, Cigar Butt George to my left, and Ivan at my 1:00. Each of us drew a card to see who'd deal first. I got the Queen of Spades. Skinny George drew a deuce, the lowest, so he grabbed the unwrapped deck and began shuffling. Ivan opened one of the other decks, took some of the superfluous cards out, and started shuffling too. "This is how we do this," he said when I looked at him. "Keep it moving."

I sized up everyone's chips. Mine was the third-biggest stack. Skinny George had the biggest. I'd bought in for $300.

"Good luck y'all," Cigar Butt George said as Skinny George sent the cards around.

"Hold 'Em," said Skinny George

When my cards came I saw 10-8 off-suit.

"To you Chief," Ivan said.

I folded.

The action went to Cigar Butt George, who without hesitation pushed all his chips in.

"All-in."

"Wow," I said "You don't mess around. Jesus."

No one laughed.

Skinny George and Ivan folded. Olive Branch George, however, said, "Call," and pushed his chips in to match the bet.

"I had less than you right?"

Cigar Butt George nodded, and said, "Push 'em all in."

He did, and sat back and stared hard at the table. Since the stacks were close to equal, the call meant that on the very first hand one would be forced to buy in again. Some guys had that strategy right out of the gate: go big early, try to get a double-up you can use to bully people, buy back in if it doesn't work out, repeat as necessary.

They turned their cards up.

Cigar Butt George: Ace-Jack off-suit.

Olive Branch George: a pair of fours.

The cards took care of Cigar Butt George, who improved to a full house.

"Gotcha," he said, smiling, raking the chips in with his Cro-Magnon hands.

"Well," Olive Branch George said, "that's it for me, I guess."

He tightened his mouth in a polite smile, got up, and walked out.

No one said anything. I couldn't believe it. Was he just a sweetener? Was he an Andrew?

We sat there and listened to him fuss with the ladder, until it came back over alone.

Ivan looked at me, and nodded at the cards. "Clear the table and shuffle." he said. "New deal coming."

Hold 'Em was the game of choice, though Ivan called the occasional single-deck blackjack run-through, which was good for a few rounds. Skinny George and Cigar Butt George called Hold 'Em every time. When it was my turn to deal I called all kinds of games: Five Card, Seven Card, Draw, Stud, Black Mariah, Baseball, Black Mariah Baseball, No Peekie, Acey Deucy, Baccarat, Hi-Lo, High Spade in the Hole, Nebraska, Challenge, Waterfall. They all knew the rules to every single one.

I bluffed Ivan, emboldened by a trace of impatient energy (he sat back too fast after checking). One hand after that, I was bullied into giving up my own blind by Skinny George, who bumped hard at $100 after Cigar Butt George's fold. That play seemed like overkill given the situation. I wasn't sure. Skinny George was the hardest read—no intimidating talk, no gloating, no whining over bad luck, no idle chatter, and he hadn't turned up many cards for the table to see. For now, he was the one to stay away from.

I realized I was getting hooked into playing. Truly, it'd started the moment I turned from the ladder and appraised my new friends. Rationalizations had been brewing ever since: stay sharp, make them want another game, it doesn't affect your plan, you can abandon your plan, the silence in the room makes me comfortable and escorts me to a natural settling in, a slowing down, so I can watch, operate from an unknown place, decipher, confuse, outsmart, it's what I do, what I'm good at it, I can't help it, I won't dilute it, it's my bread and butter, my lifeforce, my raison d'etre…

–

Ivan kept looking toward the street whenever footsteps came by or cars passed. He had nervous energy. Was preoccupied. And in his play he was unaggressive, reluctant even. Lots of folds, few raises, playing the cards and not the opponent as the saying goes. He wasn't at all the guy I remembered from the casino. He didn't do anything to seem like a threat.

–

The sun sank. Ivan lit more candles, and more shadows flickered on the walls, our faces.

–

A flurry of rain came through. Wind picked up. Branches tapped at the windowpanes. A little water trickled into the cottage.

"You gonna play there?" Skinny George said to Ivan, in a crisp tone.

"I'm thinking," Ivan said, staring at the middle of the table.

"Philosophizing, seems like."

No reply. Then a quiet fold.

Cigar Butt George, who never did win another hand after the big scrape to open, busted out playing deuces against Skinny George. "Aw, it's a tarnational disgrace!" he said after the last card didn't save him, and shoved all the chips toward his conqueror with disgust. He remained with us, though. Didn't mention taking off or rebuying either, just kind of settled into a quiet spectator's role.

My stack was a little smaller than that of Skinny George, who I still hadn't taken. But I was up. Ivan was almost out, mostly because I'd been beating him every time we went head-to-head. Skinny George was beating him too. Ivan got me on the next hand though, flipping over Queens connected to one on the board. The take made us almost even, but he didn't gloat, only scooped the chips in quietly.

"I need a drink," I said, shuffling while Ivan dealt a new hand.

"Second that," said Cigar Butt George.

Ivan looked at us but didn't say anything. Again I wondered what changed his demeanor so much.

Cigar Butt George went out to get alcohol and cigarettes, and, he said, another buy in for himself. That last detail bothered me. I wanted to finish them all off, get their money and get to the next phase of the plan. Or did I? Did I want the game to go on, and watch Ivan get tired? Did I want to *throw* the game? Was this the same setup I was looking at in Andrew's game? Were they dangerous? Should I run now?

Before the next shuffle went around, I decided I needed a moment. I wanted to see where Ivan was at, gauge how formidable he seemed. Plus it had gotten stuffy. I turned and saw him collecting cards from the last deal with a blank look on his face. "Can we take a few minutes?" I said. "I need to stretch my legs. And I need to ask you about something."

"So ask."

"I just told you, I need to stretch my legs," I said. "Can you come out with me?"

Grudgingly, he put the cards down and got up. Skinny George was looking at cards he'd been shuffling himself. He showed no reaction to us. Didn't even look up, just kept shuffling.

Outside the air was less stifling than in the shed, but not by much. The rain's aftermath was omnipresent. You could hear trees drip. The ground smelled like wet cement.

Puddles shone with moonlight.

We walked toward the main path, but before we got there, Ivan stopped me in a slovenly walkway squishy with mud. "What is it Chief?" he said. "What do you need?"

I paused.

"Ivan, when will we go to the casino?"

"You ask me this now?"

I looked at the shed.

"Chief."

"Ivan," I said. "How do you know these guys?"

"I don't," he said. "Friends of friends. That's it. Simple."

At that, he headed back inside. I couldn't think of how to stop him, so I just stood and watched.

Insects buzzed all around me. I imagined thousands of their little eyes sizing me up for a landing place:

fireflies   roaches   mosquitoes   roaches

roaches   gnats   junebugs   roaches   gnats   moths

termites   gnats   roaches   grasshoppers

       roaches   ladybugs

The fusty atmosphere forced us to open a window, but just a crack, since we had no screens. Every so often a roach got in. Ivan would always hunt it down. Termites got in too, but they just kind of fluttered up into the darkness and vanished.

A spider crawled across the papered window behind Skinny George.

Outside I heard an airplane, flying low. A car.

Ivan posted the blind.

I dealt. "Hold 'Em," I said.

They were so quiet. Dead silent. Ivan's chips sounded like something shattering when he threw them into the pot.

"What took so long with all this?" Ivan asked when Cigar Butt George returned with our treats.

"The one across the way was closed."

"The 24-hour one?"

"Yup. Had to go to 1st."

Cigar Butt George sat down, grabbed some cards and started shuffling them. Was he doing that before? "There were guys out in front of the market," he said, "talkin' about Betsy."

"Who?" I said, reaching for a beer.

"The old storm."

"Oh."

"Remember Betsy?" Ivan said. "Debris in brick walls one inch deep."

He held his thumb and index finger close together and smiled at me. Skinny George looked at him a moment, went back to shuffling his deck.

Cigar Butt George didn't buy back in, like he said he'd do.

-

Around and around the deals went, the luck moving back and forth pretty even. I gained an advantage by locking in on Ivan, who'd become more inclined to frown at bad cards, wait for his turns with varying levels of patience. I wondered if Ivan was trying to tip off Skinny George, and watched the latter for responses to Ivan's movements. But I wasn't seeing anything.

Minutes later I stung him with a set of threes and reduced him to a tiny stack. "Crapper snappers!" he said, throwing the cards down. He thespian rage seemed wholly artificial to me. It wasn't that reflexive buffoonery that comes out when he's really mad. I sensed a façade.

On the next deal, he looked at his cards and put them back down immediately. "I'm all-in," he said, and sent all his chips into the middle of the table.

Skinny George folded.

"How much is that?" I said.

"Less than you have smart guy."

I looked down at my chip stack to count out what would match him, and for the first time, noticed that on the back of my cards, the circle in the middle was blue on one card and white on another. My Ace, but not my King.

Ivan's cards didn't have any dots, so I called.

I busted him. He didn't say a word, only went outside to smoke a cigarette.

Now it was just me and Skinny George. Who else knew about the dots? No one? I was afraid to make an accusation. My best guess was they had it as a failsafe, something in case the going got rough. But that didn't sound right. If they'd marked the cards they'd have exploited that a long time ago.

Cigar Butt George kept dealing in silence, and shuffling when he could. Why was he still here? I could see Ivan looking after the place, but what was his interest? I thought about this. Roles emerged: Ivan as the coordinator, Cigar Butt George as the muscle, Skinny George as the best player. Probably the ringleader.

-

Skinny George's cards both had dots.

I folded.

-

I won a big hand, matching ladder bets from Skinny George all the way to the river then outkicking him for the pot. It was the first time I'd taken him. Afterwards he shot a tiny eye glance at Cigar Butt George, who didn't respond.

I was tired, nauseous, ready to stop. No one had mentioned just ending the game where we were at. I thought about broaching it. Were they really trying to cheat me, or win fair and square so nothing criminal would have to occur? Maybe they were competing to see who'd get the prize and if I won they'd attack me and divvy up everything.

Wind gained strength. Leaves rustled. Branches struck the windowpanes.

-

I had Kings off the draw but didn't bump.

Two deuces came on the flop, and an Ace. Skinny George had dots on both his cards, so I folded. He took the chips in with a grave expression.

-

"You got a girl?" Skinny George said, studying me with his little eyes. This was the first time he'd addressed me all night.

"Yeah," I said.

"What's she like?"

"Cream of the melting pot."

"The what?"

"Ha!" Ivan said. "You know what melting pot means? I don't know where you came from or what you brought with you, but maybe the germs can be boiled away!"

Ivan. He was getting back to his jovial, annoying self.

Kings came to me again, and again I saw Skinny George with two dots. I knew then they'd given up on a real victory, and that I was screwed. Cigar Butt George would just keep feeding Skinny George and I wouldn't be able to detect the sleight of hand. That was impressive, in all honesty, because I'd been keeping my eyes on his shuffling and still couldn't see it. He wasn't such a simpleton after all.

I folded again.

On the next hand, for the third straight time I saw Skinny George get two Aces. They'd had enough. The trap wasn't set, it'd been sprung. We were done here.

They all were holding still, watching me. So there it was. Checkmate.

This wasn't something I was just going to take though, or flee from. It was probably the alcohol and agitation talking more than anything else, but in that moment, the tiniest bit of pride rose up and burst inside me. I decided that if I was going to get cheated, I at least could have the satisfaction of calling them out, of letting them know they weren't sneaking shit by me.

I checked my cards a second time, looked up at them, nodded, leaned back, took a drink.

"The thing about poker," I said, "there's always a reason for optimism. So many things can turn in an instant, and you think maybe, this time, things might actually work out. No matter how many bad deals you get. That's the gambling mentality. The odds are shit, but the payoff is big. And sometimes you can manipulate it. And isn't that what we're here for?"

"Enough with the talk, Chief," Ivan said. "Play game."

"Play? You all have been playing real quiet, here."

"Eh?"

I stood up and pointed to Skinny George. "I'm all in," I said. "But if this piece of shit is holding two Aces, yet again, I swear to God I'm burning this gopherwood shack down to the ground with all of you cheating assholes inside."

I reached across the table and flipped over his cards.

There they were.

He glared at me.

"Slithering your way to victory, huh?" I said. "Some player."

He stood.

So did Cigar Butt George.

As they came for me, Ivan, surprisingly, streaked to get between us. "No, no," he said. "He's the Chief, he's alright! He can't afford stitches!"

I threw a sorry punch that got blocked by the massive arm of Cigar Butt George, and was taken to the ground. The table flipped over. Cards, chips, bottles and candles went everywhere. It seemed like Ivan fell on top of us too, because the pile got heavier.

I was pinned, suffocating, writhing. I smelled their sweat. Heard their breaths. Someone was striking my head.

Bottles clanked and rolled, dust kicked up. No one spoke.

17.

Don't waste time on the question of trend or rough spot. You drown if you don't move. Or get swept away. When you do move, you don't know what will cross your path. But you have to. Sink or swim, rise or fall. *Move.*

They say God often appears to prophets in depleted landscapes. Maybe that's because fertile soil has a tendency to distract. Maybe you're invested in the spirit of a city.

The eternal in the internal. The internment of the eternal, internally.

What half-assed pontifications. Some job I was doing creating an archive, a belief system. The concepts barely made sense, and attempts to fuse them exposed all kinds of incompatibilities. Like a giant tree emerging from the ocean, rising beneath my feet as I sank.

My French line came first. Over from the old country, on to French Ohio, down the river to Acadia. They farmed and traded their way to the big city, slowly. Didn't really prosper once they got there. My great-grandfather, who we called Granddad, was a cab driver in New Orleans. Granddad used to say *his* father pulled out rotten teeth with pliers and swished whiskey in his mouth as a disinfectant. Worked for the WPA, helped build the cornstalk fence on Royal. Low level guy. Granddad was not far fallen from the tree, so to speak. After two years of safe driving the city gave him a certificate and a pin, and that very night, so the legend goes, he drunkenly spun his cab out in the rain and crashed it onto the mayor's lawn with a passenger in the back.

He married young, at sixteen I think, fathered a child around the same time. Eventually he took his family out of New Orleans and went east, west when he joined the army. Forces beyond him drove this, obviously. He wasn't moving of his own free will.

I remember a family gathering in California, one of the few personal memories I have of him. Granddad was sitting quietly in a rocking chair, watching television, as much a piece of furniture as the chair itself. Per my father's orders, I brought him a new beer, and just my luck, it was during a lull in the game.

When I gave him the beer he looked up at me with pale blue eyes that seemed to recognize me for the first time. "You're in it," he said, "you know that. Wherever you are." And then he turned back to the television, receded into his solitude.

I stood there confused. To save me, my uncle made a joke—Granddad was cranky because of a losing bet, which he ought to be used to by now. We all laughed (except him), and I sneaked away.

I still can't see the wisdom in what he said. Maybe he was senile. Or an unlucky gambler. Maybe just a drunk.

But then again, Granddad could have been an apple removed from a tree, fallen, disintegrated, seeds blown
about.

18.

They'd taken it all, the candles, money, chips, cards, cigarettes, beer, liquor, and left me in the mushpot. Nothing here besides furniture. Feeling sore and bruised all over, with another vicious headache, I stood, righted myself, checked for blood, cuts, cracked ribs, and for some reason started setting the chairs back up.

Outside, footsteps came down the sidewalk. Murmurs. I crept to the window and tore a bit of the newspaper. An NOPD car was parked, with one wheel on the curb. Some officers at the gate fussed with the lock. I retreated to a corner, knowing if they were responding to a noise complaint or if Ivan had reported me as an intruder, they'd come in to investigate. But that wasn't it, apparently; after a minute or two, they drove off.

The sky was black. Rain fell lightly through warm, damp air. The copper-colored streetlights were on, but every home, aside from porch lights, was dark. I saw no pedestrians anywhere, or traffic, and no cars parked on either side of the street.

By the time I got to the apartment complex the wind had really started to move. Ivan's unit, like every other unit, was dark. His truck was gone. Door locked. I went to the storage area, and found the door unlocked. I looked for my chips but they were gone, except for a few in one of the five hiding spots I'd made (in an empty paint can, about $200 worth). I pocketed the chips and came back out and peeped into Ivan's front window. Everything dark. No movement inside.

I kicked at the door. Looked around. Kicked again.

Before long the wood started cracking.

Blood was everywhere: drops, streaks, smudges, on the kitchen counter, the bathroom door, the coffee table, the box of candles on the coffee table. I took grocery bags from the kitchen cupboard, went to the little bedroom closet, and started bagging up the jewelry. It took three to get it all, and I triple-bagged each. After I was done I sat on Ivan's bed and tried to figure out what had happened. One possible scenario was that Ivan was cut, they all came back here, and eventually, after realizing the severity of the wound, the Georges drove Ivan to the hospital in his own truck. Or he drove himself. He knew I'd be back and left the storage room open so I could see the chips were gone and I was persona non grata. But he didn't figure I'd get into his place. That didn't explain why there was no blood in the shed though. Was there? Was he attacked *here*?

The wind grew violent. Windows rattled hard, and the walls shook.

I don't know if it was the assault, the drinking, the

stress, the hunched-over position of my body for so long, but all of a sudden I felt upwellingly sick. With a gurgling stomach, I got up, stumbled to the bathroom, and made it just in time. After flushing the toilet I lay back on the tiles and closed my eyes. Listening to the refilling water, and the storm, I told myself I'd take a few deep breaths and rest a second, just a second, then get up and go.

19.

For a while my Czech line hid in Cedar Rapids, a magnet for my people but where tradition, they said, didn't always flower. For some it did, but for others a prevalence of foreign entities fostered newness. Thus things changed. Or were modified. The Day of Love became Valentine's Day for instance. All Souls' Day became Halloween. No more Christmas carp.

My grandmother told me that nobody's ever really at one with anything. Even in a family you're alone, she said. She also said to settle means to build a home, to live in a safe place, one that might be part of a neighborhood, or city. You stop moving horizontally so you can move vertically, and you call that security, but no matter what, no matter how much you adapt, assimilate, shelter or nest yourself, you're heading toward the same thing as someone with no such concerns, no such prosperity, no customs, old or new.

When one of her brothers joined the military he got stationed in Southern California. After a few months he wrote to say that everyone should come on out. It's wide open here he said, all kinds of things are going on. Lots of business. The weather's better. And there was the water.

Not long after this he was called overseas, and no one ever heard from him again.

20.

I stood in front of the TV watching shiny-haired newscrackers report that Hurricane Noah would probably miss New Orleans, but not by much. They showed a repeating clip of the storm moving around and around like a spinning record and Southeast Louisiana was the needle. All of Orleans Parish had evacuated they said, gone west toward Houston, north to Memphis. Forecasters expected the storm would curve into Alabama, but even its edge would have enough strength to give the city yet another test.

The sickness bubbled again in the pit of my stomach. I went back to the toilet for more detox. When I was done, I went to the sink and rinsed out my mouth, splashed water on my face, saw my pale skin, red baggy eyes, thicker beard.

-

A man stood at the streetcar stop, about thirty yards away. A still silhouette. He seemed to be staring at me. Goddamn, I thought, not ten steps from Ivan's door and a threat's out there, lurking. Would he follow me back in? Push through the door? Was it Skinny George?

Wind shook the oak trees. I looked up at them, saw beads swaying in the branches. Probably got stuck there during parades.

Up the street, headlights appeared. The car moved slowly, turned right on 6th, and headed in the direction of the cemetery. That was good enough for me—it was time get the hell out of here.

I looked back to the streetcar stop. The man wasn't there anymore.

Across the street, the big church was dark. Its front windows were boarded up. Sandbags surrounded it. The windows on the side facing 6th weren't boarded, though, and some trees looked close enough to them I thought maybe I could climb one and break in. If I got inside and an alarm went off, I'd probably have some time to flee before police came. There was the possibility of a silent alarm, or someone inside. And no matter what, I'd leave fingerprints. But I couldn't stay here.

I left the apartment as I found it, aside from a front door that wouldn't close now.

-

The church's front doors, unsurprisingly, were locked. I went around to the side like I figured I'd need to, got a rock from the ground, and threw it into a window by the sturdiest-looking fichus. The shattering glass sounded like a nuclear bomb. I looked around, waited for an alarm, people, sirens.

I climbed the tree, threw the bags of jewelry into the

church, took off my shirt, swabbed my hand, punched away shards of glass in the frame. When I ventured in, I slipped on the windowsill and spun head-over-foot, and made a hard thud onto carpeted ground.

I caught my breath, felt myself out. Everything seemed to be okay. My back hurt a little. Was I bleeding? No. Nothing broken except the glass all around me.

—

I took some cushions from pews in the main area and arranged them in the center of a small room by the front door.

The room was empty except for pictures on the walls, some long folding tables at the far end.

A plan was needed. Badly. But my body hurt. Had to sleep. Was saturated with loosening tension, groggy exhaustion.

Outside the trees wheezed, sighed. Shook leaves. Sounded like waves sometimes.

We took the 71 to the 21 and went on through the greenbrier.

The Ouachita Mountains surrounded us.

On the 165 tall pines swayed near power lines, just outside Strong. Tight greenery made the road feel narrow, but then the land opened, and we saw siloed farms, forested horizons, distant clouds that were like huge crashing

waves, rumbling toward us.

In one lot trailers were painted Go USA colors, had flags, barbecues.

Monroe. Markets, shops, coffeehouses. Killfish, according to the radio, swam in local streams.

On the 49, the trunks of pine trees passed by like spokes on a wheel.

A doomed region. Saltwater creeping in and killing the marshes, all the canal-work washing soil out to sea. Some exchange program.

It all seemed automatic in replay. The first night in town, a game in La Place, little migrations toward murky opportunities. And there were other cities, the road, journeys toward prosperity, obligation, destination, destiny.

A jolt of anxiety woke me, some kind of internal defibrillator.

It was light out. The trees were quiet, wind-wise. But I could hear birds:
Loons

Grebes

Cormorants

Ibises

Spoonbills

Teals

Doves

I felt sore all over, in need of more rest. But unsafe. When would police, church caretakers, random vagabonds appear? Who'd notice the window?

Outside, a good amount of tree-wrack blanketed the avenue. Green carpet in each direction.

In the parking lot across the street, Ivan's truck was still gone. Good. When he found out I had his corpse treasure he wouldn't be thinking of me as some fleeced mark to discard anymore. I knew I needed to stash the stuff until procuring a means of cashing it all out. I definitely couldn't be walking around with it.

Where to put it? I strolled around, looking for places.

Small grates were on each side of the church's front steps. About the size of a license plate. I knelt and looked through one.

21.

On a bus out of Jacksonville, a place I had no reason to visit other than to reach the far end of the interstate, to finish the journey from one ocean to another, I got an idea to stop in New Orleans. I'd thought about heading in when I passed it on the interstate and saw the skyline, the boats, the bridge boats went under on their way out to sea. Why not? It had a casino, and it's where some of my family once lived. Maybe some still did. I could find them. Van Matrie, was the last name. If I found them I'd be accepted by default, right? Taken in?

I knew I couldn't stay where I was, that was for sure. In fact I never could. When I had a feeling people knew I was walking around with money, I knew I had to go. And when I was down, I did things that made an expedited departure all the more necessary. Always. Always the same patterns, the same endgame. Over and over.

My family's wealthiest line was the Welsh one. Three generations ago they came to Southern California via Panama. Only my mother remained, and most of what I knew about them came through her. Money set them in their ways, she said, their customs, stuffy practices, tendencies to sermonize. That's the way it is when you're secure, she said. You think of your comfort as a byproduct of superior judgement.

I remember a black-and-white of my grandfather that we kept propped up on an end table in the living room. In the picture he's down on one knee, in front of a flag, wearing his uniform, smiling, his gaze fixed on something well above the cameraman's shoulder.

Less than a year into his time overseas, an explosion would burn his hands so bad he'd have to come home. He couldn't use them for months, but as my mom said he liked to say, it was damned good fortune.

22.

Roach on my leg. Twisting antennae, longer than its body. I slapped it into some leafery.

Any more?

In New Orleans, this wasn't such an uncommon thing, but it always pissed you off, and now it served as a reminder outside was not a good place, as if I needed another one.

I got up.

-

I picked a house in the middle of a dark, dead block. I found it locked—doors, windows. Down the side and in the back, more of the same.

Across the street, a light came on. Footsteps made wood creak.

"We've got martial law right now," a man's voice said. "And ain't the good lord gonna keep you from my gun!"

I ran through the backyard, crawled over a fence, made my way into an alley. Three blocks later I ducked between two houses and stopped beneath a massive elm tree, listened for footsteps, caught my breath.

A low-slung bungalow's front yard was pocked with weeds, tall grass, mud, leaves, branches. The roof was missing shingles. Overgrown bushes infested the porch. Like the church I'd broken into, its front windows were protected by plywood. On one board someone had spray-painted ISAIAH 43:2 in red.

I went down the side. Took off my shirt, swabbed my hand, waited for the first noise. When a plane passed, I broke a window.

The fridge had nothing but bottled water inside. Cupboards were bare. I drank some water, and went into the living room. This room felt a little strange: a stopped grandfather clock stood next to an empty fireplace with nothing on its mantle but candles with white wicks. Several crookedly-hung pictures were next to the clock. One was a black and white of a high school band. All boys. The name Marshall's Marauders was on the bass drum. Another picture, this one in color, showed a middle-aged man cutting a frowning kid's hair in a barbershop. Another was a picture of the same man, much older, standing in a small boat with a woman. Tied to a dock. Each of them smiled and dangled a caught fish.

Farther down, a long hallway dead-ended into an open door. I went down it, walked through the door, and entered a bedroom.

A man stood in the room, staring at me. I stepped back. So did he. My heart beat hard, punched at my rib cage, but then I saw it was me, in a giant mirror.

Jesus, I was out of it.

I took in my feral posture, soiled clothes, dirty, stubbly face. Should I take a shower? Take some clothes?

Chopper cuts. Bullets popping? I opened my eyes.

No clock on the nightstand, just another picture: same couple, on a dock, next to a sailboat. When would they return? What about vigilant neighbors? I remembered a story about some kid who'd broken into a cop's house the last time this happened. When the cop entered his own house and saw the kid there, the kid raised his arms, and took a bullet anyway.

Saint, Tiger, and Green Wave paraphernalia decorated another bedroom. No clothes in the closet. No computer or TV. Bare desk. Made bed. Was the kid away at college? Something worse?

Outside, from what sounded like a long way off, a wretched noise rang out, something like the screeching of metal, a train stopping out of emergency. I paused, waited for more of it. Nothing.

What would do that?

I went to the kitchen, took out some water bottles, wiped the handle, opened the back door, and wiped both doorknobs.

The neighborhoods changed personalities: smaller homes, more window bars, every yard with a fence, side gates topped by barbed wire. No lights were on in any place I saw. I chose one randomly, approached it, peered through the windows.

Turned around, scanned the street.

The place had a strange odor, like the smell of wet fur. Was a dog here? No, I would have known that immediately. Maybe it was dead.

Natural light shone at the end of a narrow hallway. I went toward it, and entered a kitchen. Two vultures were perched on the sink, next to an open window. Huge birds. Sharp, compact beaks. Feathers the color of dried blood. They looked at me like I'd interrupted a conversation.

"Look at you!"

Between two houses, a middle-aged man sat on a side stoop in shorts and a tank top. Ten steps or so from the sidewalk. He had a small turkey on his lap. Or a large chicken. Wasn't he worried about bugs?

"How are you?" I said.

"Sacramento's the most flood prone city," he said. "That's what they say. You believe that?"

"Huh?"

"Where you headed?"

"Hell in a bucket."

He looked at me.

"You hungry?" he said, holding the thing out and smiling.

"Not for that."

"Well, *alright*."

"I'm just passing through."

He didn't say anything.

I turned to walk away. When I did, he said "Alright" again, in a tone I'd call fatherly skepticism. This made me stop.

"You know," he said. "Trouble's breaking shells."

"What do you mean?"

He threw his head back and laughed, with a mouth full of poultry mush. After calming down, and laughing a little more while chewing with his mouth closed, he swallowed and said, "This is a feast day."

"Is that right?"

He tilted his head downward. I saw his eyes, peeking at me from above dark lenses. "You know," he said, "this city's end was written in 2 Timothy 3."

"2 Timothy 3?"

"One through seven. But right now, it's worse in Alabama."

"How bad?"

At that he only smiled, pushed his glasses up, and went back to picking at the bird.

I went down the street, listening for his voice, or footsteps, but hearing only buzzing insects and distant helicopters. I thought about Genia, and how the Quarter looked. The Quarter always did okay in times like these. That's why they started there. Probably should have been where they stopped. Had she left? Was her place empty too? Who knew. *Genia.* I felt like she brought the liar out of me, and I was all too happy to oblige. That probably wasn't right. Probably unfair, short-sighted, self-pitying. Whatever the truth was, I sure as hell wasn't going there now, all soiled, beaten up and short on funds. I'd tried that already.

Two blocks off of Carrolton and Canal I came upon a giant puddle that swamped a small intersection. Murky in color, dirty-looking. Had to be a backed-up drain. A huge, horseshoe-shaped apartment building was on the other side of the puddle, catty corner from me. Water pushed into its courtyard. I stood there watching it, waiting for movement.

23.

Why chance it on the highway? After shit jobs, drugs, and criminal offenses, and you discovering something you're good at and want to capitalize on? Besides that?

I owed too many people too many things, saw no advantage in a fancy tomb, had drifted from old constructions, the family, the faith, prescribed matriculations, everything but one thing.

What could I do? Did all roads lead to the garden of shadows? Did I *need* fatherly types to be absent? What would help me clear a path, forge a construct? Money, partners, women, family, games, cities, good luck, carnival? In the end, I felt, those who came before me had circled me in, and within their legacy I rose, sank, fell, drifted, passive, beaten, floating, bobbing, buried. Dirty all the time. At least I had some options, some time. Sort of.

This was all I had after shuffling my two ideas, circles and soil, cherry-picking from experience to consecrate a coda. It was a failure, the effort. No consoling illusions would flourish. It was all improvisation and half-baked secular mysticism.

When I was passed out beneath the elm tree, right after I'd left the church, I actually had a dream. I was sinking down into the canyon, with sharks swirling around me, and the sea surface vanishing, and I looked down and saw something huge coming up beneath me. Dark. Extending out in every direction for what looked like miles. Something like a giant mass of seaweed, and it met my feet, caught me. I felt a branch. Leaves. I clutched a branch as the tree pushed me upwards, toward the turquoise surface, and through the surface, and into the air, up, up, a hundred feet above the water.

Apples were everywhere. They began falling, one after another, loosening from their stems. They fell and fell by the thousands.

I crawled to the trunk and came down the tree. The sea surface was covered in apples, with more splashing down. The noises they made were deafening, like a stampede moving through a river.

Then they stopped falling.

One more.

I came all the way down to the bottom and found there were so many apples I could walk on them.

I took a step. Would I fall through? Beneath my feet, I could feel the water rolling. But I kept on.

<h1 style="text-align:center">24.</h1>

A front door opened. Laughter. Through the blinds, I saw two kids coming out of a unit across the street. Each sloshed through the puddle with large cardboard boxes. They took their freight to a nearby truck. One was a fat kid in a green T-Shirt and jean shorts; the other one, even fatter, wore regular jeans and a stained tank top.

The building was two stories high, and very long around. Empty as far as I knew. I had an upstairs place. The front window offered a view of the street and a muddy courtyard.

I'd found the inside robust with

bags of pretzels

canned produce   Parliament cigarettes

a record player   records

tax forms   health forms

a pink card   red rooster hot sauce   newspaper clippings

counseling center brochures   suicide hotline brochures

stacks of coins   jewelry

whiskey   dry vermouth

an olive jar

The walls were cracked and dirty, the rooms littered with unlaundered clothes, but the air conditioner worked. And the shower.

The kids drove off. Sometime later, a teenager cycled by,

took a pass through the courtyard which had less water now.

Dogs barked, a few blocks away. Cars went by. People came down the middle of the street and walked around the puddle that'd shrunk in size.

Dusk came.

In another unit, a light went on.

Two cigarettes later I headed out, beneath a sky that darkened as the sun lurched Pacificward.

<h1 style="text-align:center">25.</h1>

At Greenwood Cemetery a huge iron reindeer glowed in the moonlight and loomed over a hill enveloping slain firemen. A gargoyle of Canal's dead end, serving as a reminder New Orleans always angled a few degrees toward the surreal. I pressed on, down the streetcar tracks, through the pain of my bruises and tight muscles, past an alley I knew was famous for flamed-out hotwires (no cars there at present). The ground was covered by a mess of broken glass, plastic bags, wrappers, bottle caps, cans, leaves, branches.

Along Canal the trees looked gaunt and sickly, ugly, diminished by sick roots. Many of the homes they fronted were broken down, some crumpled-looking as if the air had been let out of them. All but a few were dark.

Beneath the interstate squatters ignored me, stayed mothlike near their bin fires at the overpass pilings.

Down Canal, streetlamps and buildings sent up a collective glow that colored low clouds a dull gold shade. People were out. Neon flashed and blinked. Music blared from shops. Near Rampart I came upon two loafing policemen leaning on their car and talking. They glowered at me when I walked by. Strange to say, it made me feel at ease. Amidst normalcy, maybe.

I took Burgundy down to Dumaine. Went right at the

corner market. Half a block later I came upon our blue stoop, a gnarly old thing protruding into the sidewalk with decrepit ostentatiousness. A kid sat there, a hunched silhouette. When he saw me he stood. "Lookin for that fire?" he said, and smiled. I said no and he sat back down. When I went to the left gate, he got up and walked off.

In the back every unit but ours was dark. I rang the doorbell, heard it sound out down the walkway.

In light that shone onto the neighboring wall, a shadow appeared. The lock turned. The door creaked open.

"Who is it?" she said.

"Your old roommate."

Her head peeped out.

"Oh my God!"

She came to the bottom of the steps, stopped. Glanced back inside, turned back to me again.

She wore slacks and a collared shirt. Looked sweaty. Makeup, jewelry. She'd been working. Were her parents as rich as she let on?

"Back in school yet?"

"Adam, where have you been? Are you okay? Did you get hurt again?"

She came up close. I wanted to kiss her, ask her to pretend nothing bad ever happened. Like a coward.

"I'm okay," I said. "I just need my passport."

"Your passport?"

"So I can get it all."

"All what?"

"My chips. I have chips. A lot."

She didn't answer.

Before I could think of what to say next, someone came out of the apartment. Came down the steps. *Andrew.* When he saw me he smiled and raised his hand. "Hey buddy," he said. "Ain't seen ya in a while."

"Do you want to come in?" she asked. "We're just hanging out."

I looked back at her. "I can't right now."

"Not even to change your clothes?"

"Not right now."

"Adam-"

"When I get back. Okay?"

She was silent.

"I just need my passport. That's all it'll take to set this straight."

Again she didn't reply, and I took it as the first acknowledgment of our last meeting. I started to get angry. But rather than get into that, I only said, "I mean, set it straight as far as the money is concerned."

"Do you still think he did this to you?"

I looked at Andrew again, who stayed where he was, meek, unintimidating, like a child hiding behind his mother.

"I think *I* did all this, Genia."

"Because we can all be friends. He feels terrible about what happened."

"Okay. So, can you get my passport?"

She gave me a look that threw water on whatever sort of reconciliation might have been occurring, and went back inside. Andrew went in with her, without any acknowledgment of me. Fucking reptile.

In a minute she returned alone and gave me a tied-up shopping bag. My passport was there, atop of a heap of folded clothes.

"Change somewhere else if you don't want to come in," she said, giving off a look I couldn't decipher. Anger with some trace of sadness? Maybe that wasn't it at all.

I put my hand in my pocket and took out a piece of jewelry. To me, it was the most-expensive-looking thing from the last house I'd busted into, and the only thing I'd taken: a ring with a big red stone.

I reached through the bars. She let me take her hand. I passed the ring to her and she clutched it.

"I've got access to what I owe you," I said. "I'll see you soon."

She nodded, and walked back down the walkway. I watched to see if she'd look down at what I gave her, or me, but she didn't.

A dry squall murmured somewhere in the sky while I stood there and ripped the shopping bag open. As I fussed with the clothes an envelope fell from the bag and fluttered to the ground. My name was on the front.

At the first corner, I threw it in the trash.

26.

The Quarter had a dim glow to it. Activity was sparse, compared to Canal. Music came from bars and trinket shops at low volumes—Church caroling, it sounded like, was off in the distance, by the river. I did a lot of walking, back and forth, around and around. Near Chartres and Ursulines I passed some people out on a stoop. An assortment of white kids. Their open door revealed a living room lit up by candles. They must have been new in town because they said hello and offered me a beer. I shook my head, said, "No thank you. Y'all have fun."

More young people walked up and down Bourbon. College kids, with dozens of beads on. Big beers in their hands, acting like they always did: rambunctious, oblivious, taking pictures. Up on balconies I saw diners, mostly older people, looking down at all of us the way Jello Dress did from her apartment.

I didn't see anyone looking like they were out to fleece the temporary citizenry. A few barkers were out, smiling, nodding as you passed. They didn't really count. A vampire posed on the St. Peter corner. Not far from him a silver man in a silver suit did the same. Both had cardboard boxes in front of them. Harmless.

A long walk uptown awaited me, and a longer walk back. Then what? I'd probably cash the few chips and the jewelry

I'd stashed, get food, buy a bus ticket. Where to, I had no idea. The bigger the city, the better. Houston or Atlanta. Houston was closer. Probably Houston. Taxi rides to pawn shops. No gambling for awhile.

Before setting out uptown, I needed to use a restroom. I ducked into a bar near Iberville with open doors and windows. Candlelight and dim bulbs made the place feel old, tired. Inside a few patrons looked over at me—business-casual outsiders hunched over their drinks like they were grizzly locals. No music played. I saw no bouncers. The only one who appeared to be on the clock at all was a comfortably-blubbered woman behind the bar.

When I tried to slink past her to the bathroom, she snapped to life.

"What can I get you?" she said.

I stopped.

"Look," I said, "I'm broke right now."

"Well, sir-"

"I lost everything in a poker game. Can you believe that?"

"Are you kidding me?"

"No ma'am."

She started walking toward me.

"Sir, I can't let you use the bathroom."

Someone spoke up behind me.

"You did *what*? Lost everything in a poker game?"

I turned.

The annoyingly nasally voice had come from a table by an open window.

A group of guys sat crowded around it.

Khaki Creases   Upturned Collar

Phone Camera

         Portly Boss (probably)

Hair Glue

"The truth?" I said, turning away from the grouchy bartendress. "I'm just in from a North Arkansas shelter. I live uptown."

"Ah."

They all nodded.

"How'd you end up in a shelter?" the oldest one said.

"Was out at Gulf Shores. Playing cards."

More nods. Smiles.

"Get roughed up there?"

"No," I said, and pointed to my face. "This happened at the shelter."

Some of them gave angry little snorts; it seemed to be a moment of shared derision. I clenched up my mouth, raised my eyebrows, shrugged my shoulders.

One of the kids motioned me over. "Buy you a drink?" he said.

I sat down and shook their hands and told them my

name. The kid who'd invited me over went to the bar to fetch me an Irish whiskey—when the drink came, they watched me take a sip, which made me think maybe they wanted to make a toast, so I brought my glass over the center of the table. "Here's to fringe happenings," I said. At that, they all laughed and clinked their glasses against mine, even Hair Glue, whose glass was empty.

"So a bona fide storm victim, eh?" Portly Boss said, after we'd swallowed and made hardcore faces.

"That's right," I said. "So that makes this drink part of the relief effort then, doesn't it?"

They laughed.

"What are y'all doing in town?" I said.

"How do you know we're just visiting?" Hair Glue said.

"Come on."

Silence.

"Actually," Khaki Creases said. "We're on a weekend break from helping out in Mobile Bay."

"That right?"

He nodded. "A furlough you might say. In town til tomorrow."

"Where you from originally?"

"Oklahoma."

"Get out of here."

"Really!"

Outside, two young women walked by. I elbowed Portly Boss, who looked over. The underlings noticed, and looked too. They all chuckled.

"So, it's a mess out there in Alabama?" I said.

"Well, not only that," Hair Glue said, "we're short on personnel."

"Oh yeah? What kind of personnel?"

"All kinds. That's a long-term operation too. Damage goes far inland."

Upturned Collar said, "We're on our way to the casino right now. Hold 'Em tables."

I became transfixed by this revelation. *They play poker.* That might not have been a good thing to follow up on though, an angle best left alone. Or was it?

"So I'm guessing you're not part of a church effort," I said.

They laughed.

Portly Boss said, "Wanna go with us?"

"Do they really need bodies in Alabama?" I said.

He looked surprised.

"No I meant go with us to the casino."

"Oh."

"You interested?" said Khaki Creases.

"In the casino, or Mobile Bay?"

They laughed again.

I decided to press the issue. Maybe, I thought, I could get myself straight in a place like that, figure out a plan. A bus ride to Houston seemed depressing, and really, would pawning the shit I had be that simple? Maybe Ivan was having trouble pawning it himself, the reason why the pile was so big. And there was another maybe: someone had found what I'd stashed at the church.

"Seriously," I said. "Could I get set up out there if I wanted to?"

"Let's talk about it at the tables," Portly Boss said. "You all ready to lose?"

"Dude," Hair Glue said, "he's a storm victim, he can't play."

They looked at me for a ruling on this.

"Well," I said, "that's true. But if you need bodies out there, I can help. I'd need to hitch a ride though."

"What, out in Alabama?" said Portly Boss. "You really want to?"

"Not much here to occupy my time lately," I said.

"You don't work?"

"I help out with my father's business. He lives uptown."

"What business is that?"

"Real estate. Slow market right now though."

They nodded.

"So what are you doing walking around here without any money?" Portly Boss said.

"Honestly, I'm in a tiny apartment uptown, and I just wanted to get the hell out for a couple hours."

"See if anyone'd buy you a drink?"

"Maybe. It's hard to get that lucky," I said, smiling.

No one laughed.

"Well," Portly Boss said, after some uncomfortable silence, "I guess you could come on out. It'd at least make us look like we did something productive when we were here."

"So do you think I could get a ride then?"

The kids all looked at their leader.

"We're heading out tomorrow," he said. "About seven. Our hotel's on St. Phillip and Royal."

"Okay."

"But you'd need a ride back. And if you want to switch sites, you'll have to work that out on your own. Can you handle that? You familiar with all that?"

"Yes sir," I said. "I sure do appreciate it."

"How come you don't have your own car?" Hair Glue said.

"Long story."

"Well, it's volunteer work out there," Portly Boss said. "They'll give you a trailer, some meals, but that's it."

"That's fine."

After a little more small talk they stood up, and I shook all their hands, thanked them for the drink, wished them luck at the tables. I felt maybe they were trying to get rid of me, get away from me, but the youngsters seemed alright. I turned around and saw the bartendress, two glaring eyes atop a glacial heap of lard. I didn't know what I'd just brokered, or if they'd be there, or what they thought of my story. In any case it was time to go uptown.

27.

Rain fell hard through the orange lamplight.
Royal, colossal Canal, then St. Charles. Pushing along
I stared at myself in each reflective surface, looking for the
flower of the lily of the valley.

-

More was there than I remembered. My pockets couldn't
hold it all. $220 in chips. I decided to take the chips, cash
them, and come back for the jewelry.

Ivan's unit had light on. No others. His truck was down
in the parking lot. I went by fast, staying on the opposite
side of the street.

Half an hour later I reached the casino. Dripping wet,
I stood atop the steps and watched a few cars pass. Soon
enough, the chips were liquidated, what was left of them
anyways. When I came back out I stared at the orange rain
and watched more cars. Not many people out. A streetcar
came down Canal, shining its cyclops headlight. Turned
right, into another loop uptown. Staring at it, I thought,
why not do that? Even with Ivan suspicious of me, or even
looking for me, and Genia despising me, why not do that?
Going to Alabama was exiling myself, and how did I know
Houston would be a better place to hock my wares?

The sky really opened up. Rain hitting the ground made frying pan noises.

28.

I was down by the river, in the mud, between rocks, laying on some, the same place I'd been before. At one point footsteps came to a stop on the walkway above me. After a moment they moved on. I wanted to go out for more pizza, a beer, but was afraid to be seen. At least it was warm out, and the rain had eased up almost right away.

I'd gone back uptown with a gym bag full of food, water, a bottle of Jameson. I got a rain slicker too. It was rough carrying it all, especially after all the walking I'd done, but I really wanted this second trip to be the last one.

After I had all the jewelry in the bag (with the church completely lit up, along with the rest of the block), I stood and turned around, took a view of things.

Across the street, a figure was on the upper walkway of Ivan's building. Holding still.

It descended the stairs quickly.

I went left on 6th, right on Carondelet, and didn't stop until I found a huge broccoli-looking elm at Jackson that gave me cover from the rain, people. I backed way up, against the trunk.

Hardly anyone came by—some kid rushing to his car, two with umbrellas who passed anonymously. In time I judged it safe to head back out.

Catfish leapt from the water. At their apexes, their bodies would reflect the orange lamplight then they'd splash back into invisibility.

<h1 style="text-align:center">29.</h1>

Seven chimes of the bell woke me up.

Beneath a slate gray sky, I got up and walked to Royal. Shivering, and keeping an eye out for Ivan's truck, I crouched in a payphone booth on the corner of St. Philip and Royal. A hotel I figured was the one my new friends had referenced and a coffee shop were nearby. No one took any interest in me. Sparrows surrounded an overflowing trashcan outside the coffee shop, and picked through trash that had fallen from it.

Taxis came and went. An empty mule carriage clopped by. I looked at the hotel, at the lamps fixed to the walls outside, their glass-encased flames, wondering if my friends would show, if they were gone already.

Finally they came out, looking droopy-limbed, slow-footed. Each of them had bags like mine.

I made my approach.

When they saw me none of them looked happy to see me, but they all gave a nod.

"Hey," I said, feeling like the type of person I always tried to avoid. "How'd y'all make out?"

"Ehh." Hair Glue said, in more of a grunt than a reply. The others chuckled like gurgling doves.

Portly Boss came lumbering out of the lobby, a giant leather satchel on his shoulder. We all looked over at him.

When he saw me, he said "Hey there" in a flat tone that sounded polite and rude at the same time.

"Hey," I said. "Still got room for me?"

He rubbed his eyes. "You really coming out to work?" he said, staring at the ground with wide eyes and blinking a few times before looking back at me and estimating me, my bag.

"Of course," I said.

"You sure? We're taking you along knowing very little about you."

"Come on," Khaki Creases said. "He's alright."

"Yeah?" the boss said. He turned to me. "That true? You alright?"

They all stared at me. I took a breath, smiled a little.

"The thing is," I said, "I've been through enough lately to want to make some things easier for people. Any people. I don't care. And you know, right now, I've got the time."

Same as last night, the kids all looked at the boss. He checked me out a little more, seemed satisfied.

"Well then," he said, "We'll get on the road and drive for a while. Get breakfast later."

Five, including me, got into one car. I didn't know why Popped Collar would travel alone, why we wouldn't go three-three. Whatever the reason, I didn't ask, just put my bag in the trunk, got into the back seat, and, of course, ended up in the middle. It made me realize I'd forgotten deodorant. At least I'd taken a shower at the last house I was in.

As we pulled out onto Royal I started to relax, and thought about planning out my immediate future, but this only lasted three blocks. At the intersection of Bourbon and Ursuline, I saw Ivan. No one else did: the two on my sides had their eyes closed and heads against the window, Portly Boss was up in the passenger seat fussing with some paperwork, and Khaki Creases was watching traffic.

He stood outside his truck, drinking coffee. I knew he'd been looking for me. When we made eye contact it was like one of those moments when you're speeding and you go by a police officer, and by the time you think to slow down he's already pulling out to get you, with your infraction locked into his radar.

-

I waited for the horn, for the back window to shatter, for everything to go black, for him to pull up to our side, ram us from behind, but none of that happened. Did he think I was under arrest, maybe? Had he backed off? I didn't want to turn around and see—the idea of him on our tail, the *sight* of him, was too much to stomach.

Our little confederacy got onto the highway, pushed north. By the time we'd rolled over the lake and were in Slidell moving fast toward the forest, the cranky old supervisor had dozed off in the passenger seat. It was just me and Khaki Creases then, who looked ready to pass out himself.

I still hadn't turned around. Or tried to find him in the rear-view mirror. Would he lurk behind us this long? If he'd been driving around all night looking for me, I doubted he'd give up so easily. He'd be there. Unless he needed some anonymity. Maybe he'd follow us all the way to our destination, stay hidden awhile, seek his payback in a quiet way.

I had to turn. I had to know. I really didn't want to see him. *Or did I? Was it a way back in?* If he were there, and wanted to make a big scene of things, I knew any plan to stay with this crew would be sunk. There'd be no explaining my way out of it. Who knows what that would lead to, getting exposed like that?

So where did that leave me?

What if, somehow

  I got away

     liquidated all this shit, **but was**

        returned Genia's money, **always**

          and stood before her **looking over**

            redeemed and dressed up, **my shoulder?**

I started to turn, circling around with a sinking sensation inside me. I felt my body twist, like a stem on a branch. And in that moment, that twist, that feeling, I found my epiphany: any way you structure it, any pattern you fall into, any scenario you plan for, the truth is, it doesn't matter if Ivan's there, because there will always be one version or another of Ivan there. Fend him off, hide, evade, outsmart him, what would be different if he caught up to me later rather than sooner, aside from more miles, more frustration, more repetition, either him or another?

Without looking, I turned back, stared at the road ahead, the forest beyond, the sun coming up over the forest. It'd take us in soon, shadows first.

A previous version of this novella was a finalist in the Faulkner-Wisdom Creative Writing Competition, sponsored by New Orleans' Pirate's Alley Faulkner Society. Thank you to all those involved in the society for hosting so many great events (especially Rosemary James), and thank you to James Nolan, Richard Nash, and Michael Murphy for their advice on improving my work.

I would also like to thank the writers Doug Rice, Peter Grandbois, Janette Turner Hospital, and Elise Blackwell for their support and rigorous feedback.

ZACK O'NEILL's short fiction, essays, and drama have appeared in various literary journals. *The Blue Stoop* is his second book—his first, the short story collection *Zen Creoles*, was published in 2017. His New Orleans roots go back many generations (the Van Matries and the Armants), and he lived there awhile.

www.ingramcontent.com/pod-product-compliance
Lightning Source LLC
Chambersburg PA
CBHW011152190726
48288CB00010B/3278